we choose

a novel that teaches that with
free will comes responsibility

BECCA GAINES ARCHER

We Choose by Becca Gaines Archer

ISBN 978-0-9843925-1-3

To my husband, Robert,

who encouraged and inspired me to write this book,

and

to my mother, Irene, whose loving arms

continue to be for me the safest place on earth.

When life spins us around so hard it makes us fall,

Will we crumble like Humpty Dumpty off the wall?

Will we search another's soul to find a friend,

Or care more about the package that they're in?

When the one on whom we leaned walks away,

Will we stand on our own to face the day?

When someone tells us what we can't achieve,

Will we tell ourselves what we should believe?

Will our decisions paralyze us when we're wrong?

Or will we use our mistakes to make us strong?

Will we say when times are tough we've paid our dues?

Or keep on trying even when we lose?

We get to choose.

foreword

One common but famous "first question" asked of us takes place at a very early age: "What do you want to be when you grow up?" Do we really know that answer? Most likely not. Thus begins our journey, even at such a young, tender age, to dream and create our future as various messages and expectations surround the choices we need to make so our dreams and goals come true.

Each choice we make is our footstep in the sand creating our future. Choices, choices, choices—what choices have you made today? When all is said and done we are the conductors orchestrating our own music for our lives by the choices we make and the endless possible outcomes resulting from them. God has given us the power to choose, so ask yourself this question: "Is what I am doing and where I am headed in life working for me?" Is it? There is no right or wrong—it is your choice to answer.

The author and I go back many, many years, and I can say the actions, choices, and reactions to choices she's made over the years still remain consistent, steady, and responsible. I can talk about how intelligent or educated the author is, or how she was a shy, overweight teen and now a confident, trim adult. I can speak of her strong character or of her self-discipline, the kind that pushes her in the morning, rain or shine, to get up and exercise before the rooster crows. But her life, as each of our lives, begins each day with the choices she makes. The question is, have we chosen the best path for ourselves?

I can't say enough of my admiration for my friend's ability to see past the superficial BS and listen wholeheartedly to an issue, big or small, as she quietly assesses, then carefully, creatively, and concisely responds, usually leaving you in awe. As is evident in this book, she has listened to how choices are made and how we tend to skip a step, expecting different outcomes. That missed step is realizing our choices, our power, our ability to choose comes with a price—that of being responsible for our actions.

This book allows you the freedom to begin thinking about decisions you have made in the past, yesterday, and even today. Each chapter of this book exemplifies how our choices make a difference—good, bad, or indifferent—and inspires us with a sense of hope knowing that good things can happen to good people.

I am so proud and humbled to be part of this remarkable book. The best is yet to come, my friend!

Kim E. Andrews
Career Coach
Envision Career Design
www.envisioncareerdesign.com

If we tale, they will listen.

we choose

chapter 1

"**I** HATE THIS JOB!" WARREN Carlton grumbled to himself.

Still shivering from the winter cold, he hung his coat on the hook in back of his office door and sat down at his desk. Today was his six-month anniversary in his new job as a guidance counselor at Thurman High School in the Bronx. As he stared at the neatly stacked pile of papers on his desk, all of which needed his urgent attention, he remembered how excited he had been twenty-some years ago when he decided to pass up an opportunity to go into the corporate world to become a teacher in New York's public school system. Twenty-three and fresh out of grad school, he had been full of hope and excitement about working with young people and helping to influence the minds of America's future.

Now in 2009, a man in his late forties, that light of passion had long died out and all he felt was tired and disappointed with the choices he had made in his life. He couldn't believe the years had passed by so quickly. It seemed that one minute he was a kid playing stickball with his friends in the street and a split second after it was thirty years later and he was a middle-aged man, drifting from one school to the next, hoping to find something that made him happy.

Letting out a big sigh of exhaustion as he did every morning before starting his day, he slowly began to sort through the heap of papers on his desk when his eyes were distracted by a piece of blue notebook paper on the floor just inside his doorway. He hadn't noticed it when he'd entered his office. He got up from his desk to retrieve the paper from his otherwise tidy floor. Brushing away specks of dirt, which indicated that he had probably stepped on the sheet of paper when he came in, he saw that it was a note addressed to him.

Dear Mr. Carlton:
I am nothing. No one cares.
If I live or die, no one would cry. Life just keeps on passing me by.
I'm just a face in the crowd, a pair of eyes.
And all I see is a system of lies.
Turns out Marley had it wrong – "One Love, One Heart" is not the right song.
It's just too hard to go on this way. I can't take this world another day.
So I say goodbye and peace to you.
And one day soon, there'll be peace for me too.

Mr. Carlton was all too familiar with notes like these. He had received many during the course of his career, but still felt a chill run down his back each time he read what was meant to be the last desperate cry of a disillusioned teenager. He wondered what had pushed this young person over the edge. Had they been dumped by their sweetheart? Divorce of parents? Had they looked in the mirror and seen themselves as too thin? Not thin enough? Too short? Too much or not enough of what had caused this kid to contemplate such a lethal step?

As he rose from his desk to take the note to his principal (standard procedure in this type of instance), his mind drifted back to his own teen years growing up in the Bronx. His father had been a merchant marine and spent most of his time at sea, coming home for short stretches here and there. Although his father sent money home regularly, it never seemed to go far enough. Being the eldest child, Warren had considered himself the man of the house when his father was away and tried his best to help his mother with raising his three younger siblings. He worked a part-time job at the concessions counter in the neighborhood theater after school and on weekends to help his mother make ends meet.

Despite Warren's unceasing efforts to fill his father's shoes when he was at sea, he had blamed himself when one frigid day in December right before his eighteenth birthday, he found his sixteen-year-old brother in the basement bedroom they shared, dead from an apparent drug overdose. The needle was still dangling from his arm. For the first time, he noticed the old needle marks that covered his brother's arms and the swollen feet that protruded from the bottom of his pant legs. How could he have missed these tattletale signs of his brother's drug use until it was too late to save him? That question had haunted him for the last thirty years.

He could still hear his mother's helpless sobbing as two men in white uniforms carried his brother's body from the house in a plastic body bag, which to Warren was merely an oversized garbage bag. He remembered that one of the attendants was smoking a cigarette and as they lifted his brother's body, a long piece of ash from the cigarette fell on top of the bag, which they plopped like a sack of potatoes into the back of the truck. Without thinking, Warren had taken off his jacket, climbed into the truck, and laid the jacket over his little brother's body.

Even after the truck pulled off, Warren had just kept standing there, watching in disbelief this painfully tragic end to his brother's short life. The icy cold wind tore through his shirt sleeves and felt like thousands of needles pricking his skin. Although he had experienced New York winters all his life, the coldness of that particular day was new to him. It penetrated his flesh and dug deep into his bones. Still, he had kept standing there, looking down the street after the coroner's truck that had long disappeared into the traffic of an ordinary day. He wondered how he had failed his little brother. What had he done or not done to allow his brother's life to end in such despair? It was at that instant that he decided that his life would end differently. He would go to college and make something of himself. He would be successful. He would make his parents proud.

The rattle of the janitor's mop bucket as he neared the principal's office jostled his mind back to the note in his hand.

chapter 2

IT WAS A SCORCHING HOT day in July 1974 when Lois Roberts sat peering from the window of the Greyhound bus that had brought her from Murfreesboro, Tennessee, to New York City. The bus let out a huge puff of black smoke as it pulled into the New York Port Authority bus terminal. Just a week earlier Lois had announced to her family that she was leaving home—going out to find her place in the world. As far back as she could remember Lois had known that she was not a small-town girl. She longed for the noise and excitement of the big city and had decided that when she became of legal age, she would move far away from her small southern town.

Lois had been a studious child and reading about faraway places was her favorite pastime. When her siblings were out on dates or hanging out with friends at ball games or parties, she could be found in the library hovered over a pile of books until her mother sent word for her to come home. She had grown to love the musty smell of old books, the coolness of the library's marble floors beneath her bare feet on hot summer days. The rows and rows of bookshelves held adventures for her that she knew she would never find within the confines of the Murfreesboro city limits. So within a few months of graduating from high school, she bought a one-way bus ticket to New York City. Having saved what little money she could from babysitting jobs and working at fast food restaurants after school and on the weekends, she decided the time was right for her to spread her wings, as they say, and fly the coop.

To her surprise, Lois' mother never said one discouraging word about her decision to leave home. To the contrary, she took Lois to the local Kmart and spent her last few dollars on a suitcase and a small bible for Lois to take with her.

"We may be poor, Lois, but you don't have to look it. No cardboard box for my baby."

Lois remembered how brave her mother had been that day as they said their goodbyes at the bus station. Along with the sadness in her eyes, Lois could see all the hope they held for her. She would miss her mother and the special times they shared. She would miss Saturday mornings pushing the grocery cart down aisle after aisle in the store as her mother loaded it with large packages of rice, beans, canned vegetables, and other inexpensive staples needed to feed her large family. She would miss Sunday afternoons peeling apples at the kitchen table while she watched her mother knead dough to make crusts for the pies they would make for Sunday dessert. (To this day the smell of yeast always conjured up for her a picture of her mother kneading dough.) She would miss the evenings brushing her mother's long, silky hair and pinning it neatly in a bun for her before she turned in for bed. She would miss home.

As she got in line with the other passengers to board the bus, Lois began to second-guess her decision to leave her family and the only home she'd ever known. Taking the first empty seat she saw, she sat looking out the window at her mother waving goodbye, alternating from one hand to the other. A part of her wanted to run off the bus, grab her mother by those magnificent hands, and stay put. After all, her mother's hands were magical. They could calm a child's burning fever with a simple touch on the forehead. They could stretch a meal for two into a meal for ten (and had done so on many occasions). They could even make fire disappear (having patted out the flames that engulfed the pant legs of her first-born who at six years old stood too close to the coal-burning stove, and nursed him back to perfect health in defiance of medical prognosis and all that was reasonable). They gave comfort and support to all who came in contact with them—never seeking anything in return. Why couldn't she just stay put and hold onto those hands forever?

Lois had always heard that before a person dies, their whole life passes before them. Sitting on the bus that day, she learned that there is another time when a person's life flashes before them—when they're about to enter a new one. Reflecting on her childhood, her family, and her mother's courage that day had given Lois the courage she needed to get on the bus that would take her on her long journey to a new life. It wasn't until many years later that Lois learned from her sister that the day she left home, her mother had taken to bed clutching Lois' high school graduation picture and lay there crying for an entire week about her baby girl whom she had gently nudged from the nest.

Lois knew she was a fighter. She had come from a long line of fighters—people who had been knocked down over and over again by life, but just kept getting up. She had made her choice; now she would see where it would take her. As she walked out of the Port Authority terminal onto the corner of 8th Avenue and Broadway, she felt light-headed both from old memories and the excitement of the new life ahead. With the flip of a coin (heads—New York, tails—Los Angeles), she had traveled from the Deep South to take root in the most exciting city in the world. She had never been outside her little hometown before. All she knew about New York was what she had read in books or seen on TV.

Standing outside the Port Authority on that sweltering hot day, Lois again flashed back on the life she had just left behind. Her father had died after a long illness when she was eleven years old. Times had been hard for her family before her father died, and after he died they got harder. At the age of thirty-six, her mother became a widow—a single parent to eight children. Lois' dad had always held down several jobs to make sure that his family had a roof over their heads and something cooking on the stove each day. Some of her earliest childhood memories were of the distinct aroma of pinto beans, salt pork, and corn bread wafting from the kitchen, and of waking up in the mornings to the sound of her mother's beautiful voice singing "Jesus Loves Me" as she stirred a big pot of oatmeal.

Lois' father was illiterate, having gone only through the second grade in grammar school. She never knew why he had left school at such an early age, and he never talked about it. Her mother always suspected that having come from a family of twenty-one children, school was a luxury that his family simply could not afford. As a boy, the only lesson life had offered her father was that of hard work that kept him bent over in the cotton fields with the rest of his family. Lois thought it was so sad that her father had never even learned to write his own name. Any time he and her mother had to sign papers, her mother always read the documents to him and he would make an X on the line for his signature. Still, despite his inability to read, her father always had work—fry cook, laborer, trash man—and he always found a way to take care of his family.

Lois had often wondered how life must have been from her father's perspective—unable to read a simple street sign, a captivating novel, his children's birth certificates, the Constitution of the United States which would have told him how all men are created equal. Although he couldn't read the signs over the doors, she had a feeling that her father had no trouble discerning which of the segregated men's rooms he should use or which entrance to choose when entering a public place in the Jim Crow South where he had been born, raised, and died. She had no doubt that in order to survive, her father had become a master at reading between the lines as he lived and worked each day of his life to support his family and reached for what bit of peace and happiness he could grab.

Old thoughts of home dashed from her brain and quickly evaporated in the stale air that seeped from the hot concrete streets, buildings, and thousands of bodies that crowded around her. Startled by an old, homeless man begging her for a quarter, Lois reached in her purse, handed him a coin, and headed up Broadway with a suitcase filled with her sister's hand-me-downs and a heart filled with hope.

No college degree.

No job.

No experience.

Lois had no idea where her life was headed, but the one thing she knew with absolute certainty was that she had no place to go but up.

chapter 3

LOIS ROBERTS ARRIVED AT WORK early as she often did to walk the halls of Thurman High School before the first class bell rang. As the school's principal, she always felt better when she walked the halls the first thing in the morning to identify any potential problems that could disrupt her planned schedule for the day. This morning the building felt unusually cold, causing her to hurry through her hallway inspection and return to her office for a quick cup of hot tea. As she sat behind her desk sipping the last few drops from her cup, she heard someone call her name.

"Good morning, Dr. Roberts. Do you have a minute?"

She looked up to see Mr. Carlton standing just inside her office door.

"Sure, Mr. Carlton. Come on in," she replied.

Mr. Carlton sat down in a faded, old leather chair in front of her desk.

"I found this note under my door this morning. I wanted to make you aware of it." He handed Dr. Roberts the piece of blue paper.

After reading the note, Dr. Roberts looked up with a concerned expression on her face.

"Mr. Carlton, can you think of any student you may have recently spoken with who seemed extremely depressed, or has any teacher referred a student to you who was in crisis in the last couple of days?"

"I can think of two or three kids. One in particular has been acting out quite a bit lately and I'm always getting calls from her teachers about her. I'll meet again with each one of them this morning to feel them out to see if I can identify any red flags."

"While you're doing that, I'll meet with all my assistant principals and the other counselors to advise them of the situation. I'll also speak with the head of security to see if the surveillance cameras picked up anyone this morning near the counselors' offices. I'll be in Ms. Johnson's classroom for teacher observation in ten minutes, so if anything changes, you know where to find me. Otherwise, let's meet back here in my office in an hour. We need to get a handle on this as quickly as possible. This is serious."

"I agree," Mr. Carlton replied as he got up to leave. He rushed back to his office to set up individual meetings with each of the three students he had in mind.

Mr. Carlton picked up the receiver and dialed Mr. Williams' classroom.

"Good morning, Mr. Williams. This is Mr. Carlton."

"How are you, Mr. Carlton? What can I do for you?"

"Can you send Mia Maldonado to my office right away, please?"

"Well, she's finishing up a math quiz right now," Mr. Williams replied. "I'll send her down as soon as she's done. While you have her, you need to speak to her about not turning in her assignments. She's missed handing in the last three assignments. She's going to fail my class if she doesn't shape up. Can you talk to her and let me know what's going on?"

"I'll speak to her," Mr. Carlton assured Mr. Williams.

As he waited for Mia to be sent to his office, Mr. Carlton made two additional calls to teachers requesting that students be sent to him in fifteen-minute intervals. These two students were Jamie Howard and Dayton Dennis. Both were seniors whom he had met with often during his brief tenure at Thurman and in fact, had met with each of them just a few days ago to discuss their plans for after graduation.

Just as Mr. Carlton hung up the phone, Mia Maldonado walked into his office. Looking past Mia through his open office door, Mr. Carlton noticed Mia's classmate, Lily McGlenn, who was obviously cutting class while she waited for Mia to meet with him. Both these students were freshmen and had been characterized by most of the school staff as "handfuls" who were constantly getting into trouble and disobeying rules. They both spent a lot of time in detention. "Mr. Carlton, did you want to see me?" asked Mia as she plopped down in the chair by his desk.

"Yes, I do," he replied. "Your math teacher tells me you are having some issues with getting your homework in."

"I didn't do my homework. So what?"

"Well, if you don't pass your math course, you're going to have to repeat it next year."

"Oh, I'll pass. I'm not worried about it. I have the rest of the quarter to catch up."

"Why haven't you been doing your homework?"

"I don't like Mr. Williams. He's mean. Besides, he gives too much homework. I have a part-time job babysitting after school for my neighbor. Sometimes she don't get home until late and by then I'm too tired to do any homework."

"Why can't you do your homework while you're babysitting?"

"Those kids are bad! I have to watch them every minute or they'll burn the house down." If Mia had a conscience, it would have told her to stop lying. Mr. Carlton knew there was no babysitting job after school. It was just another lie that she had conjured up on the spot to try to get out of trouble.

"By the way, Mr. Carlton, can I use your phone to call my mom to tell her to bring me my sneakers for gym class? I forgot them." As she spoke, Mia fluttered her eyelids at Mr. Carlton and pushed her bottom lip forward in a slight pout. But even Humbert Humbert's Lolita would have gasped in disbelief at Mr. Carlton's failure to acknowledge such a perfectly delivered flirt.

Reaching into the top drawer of his desk, Mr. Carlton retrieved a hall pass and began signing it while he responded to Mia's request.

"Mia, I can't let you use the phone for that. It's against school policy. Getting your mother to bring your sneakers is not an emergency. You have to use the pay phone in the hall."

"Kiss my ass, Mr. Carlton," Mia hissed at him. She snatched the hall pass from the corner of the desk where he had placed it, then turned and left, nearly bumping into Jamie Howard on his way in.

Mr. Carlton made a mental note to discuss Mia's foul language and disrespectful behavior with her mother. Right now, he needed to focus on trying to find out which student had written the suicide note; after his conversation with Mia, he was pretty confident that she was not the one.

Mia met her friend Lily sitting in the hallway near the entrance to Mr. Carlton's office. "Come on, let's go," Mia said to Lily as she walked up to where Lily was sitting.

"What'd he want?" Lily asked.

"Same ol', same ol'," Mia said. "I told him to kiss my ass. It ain't like I'm the only student in this school who don't always do her homework. Give me a break!"

"Girl, you're too much!" Lily giggled.

Mia and Lily were the best of friends. They had the same homeroom class and the same lunch period. Usually, when you saw one, you saw the other. They had met a few years ago when Mia and her mother moved into an apartment building in Lily's neighborhood. An only child and desperate for friends, Lily had gravitated to Mia because Mia was all the things Lily wasn't. Tall for her age, big-boned, and with a sassy attitude, Mia could easily pass for well beyond her fourteen years and often intimidated the other girls in their class. Lily was just the opposite—a frail wisp of a frame and shy to boot. Lily lived vicariously through Mia, doing things with Mia that she would never have the guts to do alone. Cutting class to grab some smokes in the school yard, as they were about to do now, was one of those things that Lily never did without Mia's coaxing.

As they exited the side door to the school yard, they felt the chill from a gust of wind that blew around the corner. It was February and neither of the girls had their coats since they were supposed to be in class, not outside. From her purse Mia pulled out two loose cigarettes, which she had purchased from a bodega on her way to school as she did each morning.

Mia loved to smoke. She loved everything about it. She loved the way a cigarette looked between her long, slender fingers which were accentuated by long fingernails that she usually kept polished in the most conspicuous colors—bright red or purple or even black. She loved the feel of the smoke as it warmed her throat and slightly stung her nostrils when she exhaled. Smoking made her feel grown up, and above all else, Mia wanted to be grown. She didn't like having to follow anybody's rules and wanted to be able to do what she wanted to do, when she wanted to do it.

"I love that nail polish," Lily said, gazing at Mia's perfectly manicured nails. Having her fingernails and toenails manicured was a weekly ritual Mia never went without. Every Saturday morning for as far back as she could remember she had been going with her mother to Rudy's Hair Salon downtown. They would have their hair done, followed by manicures and pedicures. Mia always noticed that she was the only little girl in the shop with her mom. This had made her feel grown up and important as she listened to the women talk about their husbands, boyfriends, families, jobs, or whatever else happened to be on the front burner for them on that particular morning.

"This color is called Hot Tamale. When I go to the salon on Saturday, I'll pick up a bottle for you."

Mia and Lily chatted away as they smoked their cigarettes, and when they were finished, they slid back through the side door and into the corridor. The second-period bell had just rung as they blended into the crowd of students returning to their lockers to grab books for their next class. As Mia headed down the hallway toward her locker, she saw Dr. Roberts coming toward her. As they passed each other, Mia noticed that Dr. Roberts had a very distracted and concerned look on her face.

Bitch, Mia thought to herself. I wonder who she's after now.

chapter 4

FOLLOWING HER MEETING WITH MR. Carlton this morning, Dr. Roberts had assembled her assistant principals and other counselors to inform them of the suicide note that Mr. Carlton had shared with her. She asked them to keep their eyes and ears open for anything unusual. Upon returning to her office after her first-period teacher observation, Dr. Roberts heard her phone ringing and saw that it was her direct line, which only a few close friends and family were privy to. She picked up the receiver and immediately recognized Miki's voice on the other end.

"Good morning, Lois. How are you?"

"Hello Miki. I'm in the middle of a bit of a crisis here this morning. Can we talk later?"

"No problem, sweetie. I was just wondering if we're still on for dinner tonight. I've been looking forward to getting together for some girl talk."

In light of all that had happened since she arrived at work this morning, Lois had forgotten that she was supposed to meet her best friend, Miki Shaw, for dinner. She and Miki had a standing dinner appointment the first Thursday of every month come rain or shine. It was their way of staying connected. They had missed the last couple of months, however, which was unusual for them.

"Sure, I'll meet you at seven at our usual place. See you then," Dr. Roberts replied as she rushed Miki off the phone.

She and Miki had been best friends since college. In fact, they had been roommates during their undergraduate years and had shared a studio apartment in a Harlem brownstone at the corner of Morningside Avenue and 123rd Street. The apartment was only five blocks from Columbia University where they both were students. Also, because it was a studio apartment, it was very affordable for them since they both were working their way through school and didn't have parents who were able to help them financially.

Their apartment had been too small to accommodate real beds, so the girls had each bought futons which served as their beds at night, but during the day doubled as sofas where they lounged to read or watch TV (which wasn't very often since they were usually in class, working, or studying). A small wooden table Lois found at the Salvation Army store pulled multiple duty, transforming when necessary from a kitchen table to an ironing board or a study space.

Lois and Miki had been through a lot together. She remembered that during those lean college years, there were many times when their dinner consisted of a spoonful of peanut butter and a glass of water. As she thought back, though, she couldn't remember a time when either of them had complained. They were both the first in their families to ever go to college and were just happy to have the opportunity.

Checking her watch, Dr. Roberts saw that she had only a few minutes before she was scheduled to meet back with Mr. Carlton. She hoped that by now he had had a chance to meet with his students and maybe even could identify who had written him the suicide note.

chapter 5

MIKI HUNG UP THE PHONE from her call to Lois and sat back behind her desk. If she scooted her chair back a few inches and looked through the narrow opening between the two buildings across the street, she could catch a glimpse of the East River. This was a ritual that she performed several times throughout her workday, especially when her eyes needed a break from looking at numbers.

Unlike most people she knew, Miki liked her job. She had always loved working with numbers and statistics, so she felt that becoming an actuary was the perfect career for her. After graduating from Columbia, Miki had gone to graduate school at Temple University in Philadelphia and, after obtaining a master's degree in actuarial science, landed a job and moved back to New York. Over the years, she had moved around to a few companies before finally, about ten years ago, settling into her current role in the actuarial department of a large, prestigious insurance company on Manhattan's east side. She spent most of her day buried in data and had very little opportunity to interact with her colleagues, which was exactly how she preferred it. Miki was not a person who made friends quickly. The few close friends she did have she had known for a significant portion of her life. Having always been a very private person, she rarely shared her personal life with anyone; in fact, Lois was probably the one person on earth who knew a lot about her.

For example, Lois was the only one of her friends who knew that Miki had been a child prodigy on the piano. One Saturday when she was only four years old, Miki had accompanied her mother to choir practice at the Protestant church in their neighborhood. Afterwards, while her mother chatted with a few of the other choir members, Miki sat down at the piano and began to play note for note the song the choir had been rehearsing. No one could believe that she was playing the piano for the first time.

After that, her mother arranged for her to use the church piano to practice every day after school and enrolled her in the music program at her school. Once a week her mother also squeezed out enough money for her to take piano lessons, which caused Miki's love for music to blossom. When a teen-ager, she had been accepted into New York's Julliard School of Music, but opted instead to go to Columbia and pursue what she considered a "real" profession. Despite her mother's encouragement regarding her musical gift, deep inside, Miki never believed she was good enough to pursue music as a career. Instead, she had decided to go a more traditional route. She had decided to play it safe.

Nevertheless, throughout the years, Miki never lost her love for the piano and for music in general. She loved all types of music—jazz, classical, rock, country. Music was always a part of her day; whether she was sitting at her mahogany baby grand after a long day, fingering out Beethoven's "Moonlight Sonata in C-Sharp Minor," or listening to her iPod as she combed through pages and pages of actuarial reports at work, she always had music playing around her. Her only prerequisite for the music that she listened to was that it had to touch something deep in her soul.

Having left for work in a rush this morning, Miki had no time to look for her misplaced iPod and had resigned herself to listening to the small radio she kept in her office. Suddenly, her brain focused on the lyrics of the hip-hop tune that oozed from the radio and vibrated in the stillness around her.

Don't hide from me! Look me in the eye!
I wanna know what you were thinking when you drove by.

Did you have a plan or was it just for fun
When you fired the shot that killed my son?

The stray bullet that found and killed my boy
And left him lying in the yard like a broken toy.
A shot through my dreams of the wife he'd take.
A shot through my dreams of the kids he'd make,
All parts of me that will never be.

Stop the car! Don't speed away!
I really need to hear what ya gotta say.
I need you to help me understand
Why you solve all your problems with a gun in your hand.
Do you lie awake at night and wonder why he died?
Do you think about me and the tears I've cried?

Whose child will you snatch away tonight?
Who's the next hit in your senseless fight?
An eye for an eye won't get you by
And tit for tat never brought life back.
Did you have a plan or was it just for screams,
When you popped the shot that burst my dreams?
When you popped the shot that burst my dreams..."

A cold clamminess came over Miki's skin as the rhythm of the song slowly trailed off and was replaced by the baritone voice of the radio host. For a moment, she sat immobilized in her chair by the painful memories the song had erupted within her. One of two children raised by a single mom, Miki had a younger brother, Alexander (whom they affectionately called Alexy), who was a senior in high school when Miki was a freshman in college.

Having dropped out of school to marry her high school sweetheart at seventeen, Miki's mom worked as a maid at the luxurious Plaza Hotel in

Manhattan to fend for her children. She had divorced their father shortly after Alexy was born and moved with her two children to a small high-rise in the South Bronx. They never heard from their father after the divorce and Miki didn't know to this day whether he was alive or dead.

Her mother had stressed the importance of getting a good education to both her children as far back as Miki could remember. Both Miki and her mom had been overjoyed when Alexy announced in the spring of his senior year that he had been accepted into the six-year medical program at Stanford University medical school with a full academic scholarship.

Then one evening, just a few days before his high school graduation ceremony, while running an errand for his mom to the corner store, Alexy was gunned down in a drive-by shooting. Turns out, he had been mistaken for a member of a rival gang because of the color of the T-shirt he was wearing.

Alexy's death had destroyed their mother. She had nervous breakdown after nervous breakdown and spent the next few years in and out of mental facilities until she finally died only a few years after Alexy. Miki knew that her brother's death had left a hole in her mother's heart that she simply didn't know how to fill. When her brother died in a bloody clump on the street that day, her mother had died with him—it had just taken her a few more years to stop breathing.

"Here's the report you asked for, Ms. Shaw." Miki was startled back to reality by her assistant, who stepped into her office and handed her a large binder filled with actuarial reports for her review.

"Thanks, Rita." As she took the binder, she could hear the cold wind swirling outside her office windows. She turned back to her work, and thought about how much she was looking forward to enjoying some warm conversation with Lois later that evening.

chapter 6

"HI MR. CARLTON. YOU WANTED to see me?" Jamie Howard asked as he stood beside Mr. Carlton's desk.

"Yes, Jamie. Please have a seat. First, I received the new financial aid forms that we were discussing yesterday. Take these and have your parents fill them out. Let them know they have to be returned as soon as possible. By the way, how are your parents doing? I didn't get a chance to ask you about them yesterday when we talked."

"They're fine. My dad just got promoted to detective and will be working in a precinct closer to home. My mom is very happy about that."

"How about you? Did you have a chance to think last night about which of the three colleges you're going to go with?"

"I've narrowed it down to two so far. I'm going to sit with my parents tonight and get their input."

"Okay, sounds good. Keep me posted."

"I will, Mr. Carlton. Thanks for all your help."

Watching Jamie leave, Mr. Carlton was glad to see that he seemed to be adjusting well. He had been meeting regularly with Jamie over the past few weeks after his girlfriend, whose father was in the military, had to move when he was relocated to Japan. She and Jamie had been dating since their freshman year and he had been struggling with the fact that she moved away.

Over the last few weeks, however, Jamie seemed to be refocusing on his future and had been very excited when he received acceptances from three of the five schools to which he had applied.

Two down and one to go, Mr. Carlton thought as he checked his watch. Noticing that he had just enough time to get to the teachers' lounge and pick up a cup of coffee before his meeting with Dayton, he left his office and headed down the corridor. As he turned the corner leading to the lounge, he saw a boy and girl kissing in the corner near the boys' bathroom. As he got closer, he saw that the girl was Mia Maldonado. He'd never seen the boy before and was pretty sure that he wasn't a Thurman student. When they saw him approaching, the boy scurried down the corridor and Mia bolted down the opposite corridor to God knows where.

Having witnessed this chain of events, instead of going for his coffee, Mr. Carlton returned to his office to notify security about the intruder situation. As he stepped from the hallway into the guidance counselors' office suite, he saw Dayton Dennis sitting in the outer office waiting patiently for him to return.

"Dayton, I'll be with you in a minute," said Mr. Carlton. He quickly entered his office, closing the door behind him. Once he connected with security, he advised them that someone was intruding on the premises and provided them with a description of the young man he had seen with Mia. Then he opened the door to his office and motioned for Dayton to come inside. Within a few seconds, they heard Dr. Roberts' voice over the PA system: "Attention all staff. Climb Mount Kilimanjaro!" Mr. Carlton knew that was the code to tell all staff members that there was an intruder in the building and to lock all classroom and office doors. Now that that was done, he could focus on his meeting with Dayton.

Dayton was a 4.0 student and had won numerous academic awards since grade school. His hard work had paid off and he would be graduating at the top of his senior class. His college options were many, and Mr. Carlton had suggested that he complete applications for several top schools, including Harvard, which was Dayton's "first pick" school. Dayton had dreamed of going to Harvard since the seventh grade. It was then that he had taken a tour of Harvard's campus with a few other honor students in his class. The beautiful campus, flanked on one side by the Charles River, had left an impression on him that he could not forget.

"Have you heard back from any of the schools about admission?" Mr. Carlton asked.

"No word from any of them yet," Dayton replied trying not to sound as terrified as he felt. He couldn't bear to tell Mr. Carlton that he had put all of his eggs into one basket and had applied only to Harvard. But in his mind, there was no other choice. Now it was too late to apply to any other schools. The deadline for getting applications in had already passed.

"Well, you should be hearing from them soon." Since many of the students had already heard back from their schools, Mr. Carlton was beginning to wonder what the hang-up might be in Dayton's case. He should have heard something by now.

"How is everything else going with you? Is everything on track with your classes for graduating? Everything okay at home?" Mr. Carlton continued.

"Yes, everything is fine," Dayton replied.

"Well, let me know if you need my help with anything." Just then Mr. Carlton's phone rang and he reached across his desk to answer it.

"I will," said Dayton as he picked up his book bag and left the office.

The phone call was from Dr. Roberts' assistant, letting him know that Dr. Roberts was ready to meet with him again. Well, I guess I'm back to the drawing board, Mr. Carlton thought with a sigh as he headed down the hall for his follow-up meeting with Dr. Roberts. Unfortunately, he had nothing new to report. It was going to be a long day and a night of tossing and turning if they couldn't identify the author of the suicide note soon. He walked toward Dr. Roberts' office with the revulsion of a man forced to walk the plank. Only one thought consumed his brain—how much he hated his job.

Mr. Carlton felt helpless when he left Dr. Roberts' office for the second time in one day. He'd informed her that the three students he had met with had not shown any unusual behavior or indications of being suicidal. They agreed that Dr. Roberts would follow up with the other faculty members and Mr. Carlton would meet with any other students that he thought might be in crisis.

When he returned to his office, he had a voice mail message from Mia's English teacher: "Hello Mr. Carlton, this is Ms. Ford. I'm calling to see if Mia Maldonado is still in your office. Another student told me that he had seen her in your office earlier this morning. She hasn't showed up for class. Could you give me a call when you have a chance?"

After listening to his messages, Mr. Carlton decided that he needed his cup of coffee if he was going to make it through the day. He headed down the hallway on his second attempt of the day to reach the teachers' lounge. Turning the corner to the hallway that led to the teachers' lounge he spotted Mia Maldonado, along with the head of security, in the office of Ms. Drake, the dean of students. As he got closer he heard Mia mention his name. At this, he poked his head into Ms. Drake's office.

"Mr. Carlton, was Mia in your office this morning?" asked Ms. Drake.

"Yes, I met with her for about fifteen minutes," Mr. Carlton replied. "She left my office a while ago."

"She says she left your office only a few minutes ago," Ms. Drake replied.

"No. My meeting with Mia ended over a half hour ago. I saw Mia in the hallway about twenty minutes ago with an intruder," said Mr. Carlton.

"That wasn't me," Mia angrily interjected.

"Thank you, Mr. Carlton. I'll take it from here," Ms. Drake replied, turning back to continue her conversation with Mia.

Mr. Carlton got his coffee and then returned to his office, where he spent the rest of the school day meeting with several other students, but none raised concerns for him. Afterwards, he attended a counselors meeting and then went back to his office to return phone calls and update his student files. When he finally glanced at his watch, he was surprised to see that it was close to six o'clock. He sighed. Despite where he was or what he was doing throughout the course of the day, the suicide note was like a boomerang in his brain that just kept coming back. Finally, tired and hungry, he decided to call it a day.

He stepped into the outer office of the guidance counselors' suite and was pulling his office door closed when something caught his attention. He hadn't noticed it before, since the outer office was always full of students either waiting to go in or coming out of meetings with their guidance counselors. On the floor beneath a small table in the corner of the room he saw a spiral notebook. Lifting the notebook from its hiding place, Mr. Carlton determined that one of the students must have dropped it while sitting in the chair near the table. He quickly flipped the notebook over to its front cover, and saw the name "Dayton Dennis" written in black magic marker.

He tried to suppress the sick feeling that arose in the pit of his stomach as he opened the cover of the notebook. The notebook paper was the same shade of blue as the suicide note. On the first page, he saw handwritten bits and pieces of the typed note that he had found in his office: "If I live or die no one would cry. I'm just a face in the crowd, a pair of eyes."

Quickly going back into his office, Mr. Carlton pulled Dayton Dennis' file. Then he picked up the phone and dialed the New York State Children's Safety Hotline. He explained to the representative who answered that he had received a suicide note from one of his students. The representative probed with questions: "What's the student's name and date of birth? What's the student's address? Does he have any siblings that attend Thurman? Can you give me the names of his parents?" Once Mr. Carlton had provided her with all the information, she took a brief pause and he could hear the clicking of her computer in the background.

"Okay, Mr. Carlton, we're going to send out a caseworker to the student's home tonight."

Mr. Carlton thanked the hotline representative for her help, hung up the phone, and rested his head in the palms of his hands. He reflected on the meeting he had with Dayton earlier that day and tried to recall any clue at all that Dayton was the student in crisis. He couldn't imagine why a student who had so much going for him would be suicidal. Dayton had just completed applications to some of the top schools in the country, including Harvard. He worked hard in school and had the grades to show for it. From the first time that Mr. Carlton met Dayton, he saw in him a tremendous focus and maturity that many of the other students didn't have.

Dayton knew exactly where he wanted to go to college and in which direction he wanted to take his future. He even dressed differently than most of the other students; he wore his shirt tucked neatly inside his jeans secured with a belt as opposed to wearing beltless jeans so large that they dropped down past the top of his underwear as was the popular trend. All of Dayton's teachers were impressed by him. For heaven's sake, he was one of the brightest and most well-mannered students in the school. Mr. Carlton couldn't help but wonder what could be going on in this kid's life that would drive him to the point of wanting to end it all.

After making notations in Dayton's file regarding the call he made to the Children's Safety Hotline, Mr. Carlton was finally done for the day. As he walked across the school parking lot to his car, the air felt even colder than it had that morning. He pulled the collar of his coat up around his neck, glad he had driven in to work today instead of taking the train, which would have meant a fifteen-minute walk in the cold to get to the station. He was tired, cold, and hungry and all he wanted to do was get home. As he pulled out of the parking lot and pointed his car toward downtown where he lived, his brain was still clogged with thoughts of the Dayton Dennis situation. He hoped that the caseworker would reach him in time. It would be a long night after all.

chapter 7

LOIS WAS LUCKY. DESPITE HER busy day at school, she had managed to get out of her office by 5:30, which left her plenty of time to catch a train and meet Miki in Midtown Manhattan for dinner. The Number 4 train was pulling up just as she climbed down the last step to the subway platform. Lois quickly herded herself into the subway car along with the several hundred other people who had been waiting for the train. Of course there were no seats available; there was barely enough room for her to even stand. She made her way through to the center of the subway car and grabbed onto a pole that several other people already were holding on to. She always tried to find a place away from the doors to avoid being pushed and shoved as people made their way on and off the train.

Although there were many things that Lois had grown to love about New York since she moved there from the South, riding the subway wasn't one of them. When it came to getting around in the city, riding the subway was always her last resort. However, it was still pretty heavy into rush hour and she knew that trying to take a taxi or even a bus into Midtown would take her longer than taking the train. Even on the express train, the trip would take her about thirty-five or forty minutes, so she decided to put her phobia aside and make the trip underground.

Her displeasure with taking the subway stemmed from an incident that occurred a few weeks after her relocation to New York. She was following up on a job opening for a receptionist at a company located on 34th Street near Madison Square Garden. She had taken the shuttle from Grand Central Station to 34th Street. Once she exited the train at Penn Station, she took the stairs to what she thought was the exit to outside. Instead, she had found herself in a maze of subway platforms and hallways all leading to places she did not want to go. She went up and down stairways that took her in all directions. At one point she found herself on the Long Island Railroad platform. Then she was in the main terminal and in line for a train heading to New Jersey.

To make matters worse, everyone Lois asked for directions that day had just gotten her more confused. She got so turned around in Penn Station that it took her over an hour to find her way out. She was lost in what she still referred to as the bowels of a seven-headed hydra. Since that day, the New York City subway system was a monster that Lois tried her best to avoid.

As the train crawled through the dark spider web of tunnels on its way to Midtown, Lois' mind drifted back over her hectic day. She couldn't shake the suicide note from her mind, and she hoped that the student who wrote it would not go through with his or her plan. In a situation like this one, she felt a helplessness that pushed her beyond the point of frustration. She knew that if a student seriously wanted to commit suicide, unless that student was identified, there was nothing much that anyone could do about it.

When she had days at work like the one she had today, she questioned a decision she had made several years earlier to change her career path. After obtaining her undergraduate degree from Columbia, Lois had gone to Rutgers Law School and upon graduating, had secured a job at a white shoe law firm in New York's Wall Street district. She remembered those days as both the best and worst times of her life. The pay was substantial, but so were the hours. She spent countless hours researching and preparing court submissions for partners in the firm. She pulled more "all nighters" than she cared to remember. In the legal world it was called paying one's dues, and the only thing that was important if you wanted to be successful could be summarized in two little words—billable hours.

On the other hand, working on Wall Street was more exciting to Lois than anything she could have imagined. She had a love/hate relationship with her job. She vacillated back and forth during that time in her life as to whether she wanted to continue on the legal path and try to make partner, or switch her career to one that could be more enjoyable and would allow her to maintain a work-life balance.

Her decision had come to her one Friday afternoon following a meeting with one of the senior partners in the firm—the only female partner at the time. Lois had hung around to chat with her after the meeting, and after a little cordial small talk, the woman inquired about Lois' plans for the weekend. Lois couldn't remember her response, but she was quite certain that it had not included the truth about how she spent most of her weekends. (Usually she was either in her office writing submissions for court or at home futilely trying to catch up on all the sleep she missed during the week.)

"How about you? Do you have any plans for the weekend?" Lois had reciprocated.

"Yes. My daughter is graduating from college on Saturday and I'm going to attend the ceremony. I think she's a nice young lady, but I've spent so much time working on my career that I don't really know my daughter that well."

Lois was both shocked and saddened by the partner's statement. She knew that the struggle to partnership in the legal field was demanding and one that not everyone could achieve. The conversation she had with the partner that day had emphasized the tremendous sacrifices that some people were willing to make to get there. She left the office that day with a new perspective. She couldn't help but take a long, hard look at her life and the direction she was heading.

After some honest soul-searching, Lois decided that the long, difficult trail to partnership in a prestigious law firm was not a journey she was willing to make. It was not the direction she wanted her life to take. Within a few months, she had resigned from the firm and enrolled in the education program at Columbia Teachers College to pursue a doctorate degree. Upon completing her degree, Lois had held a few assistant principal positions until landing the principal role at Thurman about eight years ago.

Just about everyone Lois knew had thought she was crazy for leaving her lucrative legal career to go into the field of education where the pay was much less than what she had been earning. Lois didn't care what anyone else thought about her choice. If there was one thing that she had learned from her arduous upbringing, it was to take control over her circumstances and not allow her circumstances to control her. Lois wanted to be happy in life, and she knew that working seventy hours a week in a job that was not gratifying for her was not the way to do it.

Although the education field was not without its own stresses, being a high school administrator provided Lois with a sense of self-fulfillment and connected her with the community in ways she had never experienced before.

She thought that perhaps her interest in working in the education field stemmed from her parents. Growing up, both her parents had preached to their children that getting a good education was critical to getting what you wanted out of life. Her mother having gone only as far as high school and her father only a few grades, her parents wanted opportunities for their children that they never had themselves. As a principal, Lois played a significant role in helping to put others on that same path.

Suddenly, the train jerked to a halt and Lois realized she was at her stop in Grand Central Station. Moving quickly, she nudged her way off the train. She followed the exit signs and stepped onto 42nd Street. She was immediately engulfed by a surge of energy that emanated from everything around her: the hustle and bustle of traffic, the large crowds of people on each corner, the shrill sound of an emergency vehicle trying to pry its way through the grid-lock. This was the New York that Lois loved. She loved the rush of energy she got when she walked down 42nd Street. It was as if her brain went into overdrive trying to take it all in at once.

For her, Manhattan was indeed a place of incongruity. From the subway, she walked by stretch limousines in front of the Grand Hyatt Hotel picking up and delivering the upper echelons of society, and just a few feet away, an old woman curled up in the corner of a building clinging to a bundle of rags that represented everything in the world that she owned.

Passing the homeless woman, Lois couldn't help but wonder what decision she had made in her life that landed her in that small corner of the world. Had it been a deliberate move, or the result of circumstances beyond her control? As Lois got closer, she noticed that the woman was holding a cardboard sign.

HELP

Please Spare Loose Change For Food

May God Bless You

The young girl who had gotten off the Greyhound bus from Tennessee years ago would have given this old woman some change. But this Lois was wiser and much more skeptical about portrayed realities. This Lois had learned rather quickly that she could find a crisis (fabricated or real) on every corner of Manhattan and she couldn't give to them all. So now she limited her giving to charitable organizations rather than to individuals on the street. She continued past the old woman, who responded by lifting her sign higher for the next passerby to read.

Lois had never regretted her decision to relocate to New York. The City had not disappointed her. It was a place of extremes where one could achieve dreams as high as the Empire State Building, or could melt into the concrete and become as inconspicuous as a queue in front of the theater. For her, it had been her salvation from the familiar, the safe, the mundane.

It had been a few months since Lois and Miki had met for dinner. Lately, they had both been so busy with their jobs that they hadn't even chatted over the phone as they typically did a few times each week. As she turned the corner onto 2nd Avenue, the pressures of her hectic day started to disappear, replaced by the excitement of seeing her old friend.

chapter 8

LYNN MARSHALL HAD BEEN IN his car heading home after a long day at work when he got the call from his supervisor. He was told that a call had come in on the Children's Safety Hotline about a Thurman High student who had written a suicide note to his guidance counselor. Lynn was exhausted and had been looking forward to getting home, having dinner, and spending the evening with his wife and ten-year-old twin boys. Having his plans changed at a moment's notice, however, was just a part of his job. So, after getting as many of the details from his supervisor as possible, Lynn turned his car around and headed to the Dennises' address in the Morrisania section of the South Bronx.

Although he had been a New York State caseworker for the past eighteen years, Lynn's heart always raced when he had to investigate potential suicides. Being a parent himself, he wanted to do all he could to prevent a child from taking such a drastic and permanent step. He couldn't imagine what it would be like to lose one of his boys, and the thought of one of them committing suicide was a concept that both baffled and terrified him. Over the years, Lynn had investigated many potential teen suicides and tried to learn all he could on the issue, and he often read books and articles to stay up to date on the subject. In fact, he had recently read an article that said suicide was the third leading cause of death among 15- to 25-year-olds and that about one-half million teens try to kill themselves every year with five thousand of them succeeding. The thought that five thousand teens kill themselves every year was mind-blowing to Lynn. As he pulled onto the Dennises' street, he hoped that he could help keep Dayton Dennis from becoming one of them.

Lynn stepped out of his car and was met by a cold blast from the night air. Although it was well past sunset, the streets were cluttered with folks arriving home from work and rushing in and out of the local grocery store and delicatessens to get dinner for their families. Lynn walked about two blocks from where he had parked his car when he saw a house with the address his supervisor had given him. The house was a large two-story row house, which even in the dim light of the evening Lynn could tell was in grave need of repairs. The only light guiding him up the steps to the door came from the neighbor's side of the porch. The porch's wooden planks creaked loudly with each step he took. He started to push the doorbell, but noticed a small piece of paper taped beneath it that said to knock on the door. After he knocked a few times, the door opened and Lynn stood facing a tall, thin man wearing layers of wool sweaters and thick wool gloves.

"Good evening. I'm Lynn Marshall and I'm from the New York City Bureau of Child Welfare. Are you Mr. Dennis?"

"Yes. I'm Joseph Dennis. What can I do for you?"

"I'm here to speak with you about an important matter involving your son, Dayton. May I come in?"

Joseph Dennis stepped back and motioned for Lynn to enter. Before the door even closed behind him, Lynn noticed right away that the temperature inside the home was not much different than the coldness he had felt outside.

As his eyes darted around the house from where he stood in the foyer, he could see through to the kitchen, where four children ranging in ages from about four to thirteen hovered around the kitchen table either reading or working on homework. They each had on coats and gloves. Several candles in the center of the table provided them with reading light. Lynn also noticed the blue flames coming from burners on top of the gas stove beneath large boiling pots that he suspected contained the family's dinner for the evening. The oven door was pulled all the way down and, as far as Lynn could tell, offered what little heat there was in the room.

A petite woman emerged from the kitchen wearing a tightly fitting black wool coat that barely hid the thick, red sweater she wore beneath it. On top of her coat she was wearing an apron that was tied at her waist and upon which she was rapidly wiping her hands as she joined Mr. Dennis and Lynn in the foyer. Mr. Dennis spoke to her in Spanish, and then turned back to Lynn. "This is my wife, Rosa. Although she understands English, she's not fluent. I've told her that you are here to speak with us about Dayton."

"Is there anywhere we can sit down and talk?" asked Lynn.

"Of course. Let's go into the living room," said Mr. Dennis as he led Lynn into a small room off the foyer. Mrs. Dennis followed them inside the sparsely furnished room. Two large candles perched on the fireplace mantel just barely glowed enough to guide Lynn to a small sofa in front of the fireplace, where Mr. Dennis directed him to sit. Large, bare windows sat on each side of the fireplace and Lynn could see towels stuffed at the bottom of each window in a futile attempt to keep out the cold air. Mr. Dennis took a seat beside Lynn on the sofa, and Mrs. Dennis sat across from them in a large armchair that even in the poor lighting Lynn could see was tattered and sagging. Mrs. Dennis' small body seemed to be swallowed up by the over-sized chair, and although he couldn't clearly see her face, Lynn could sense that she was anxious to hear what he had to tell them about their son.

"The reason I'm here," Lynn began, "is that we received a call from your son Dayton's school that he had written a suicide note to his guidance counselor. I'm here to see if we can determine what's going on."

Mr. Dennis immediately jumped up from the sofa, walked quickly to where his wife sat, leaned over, and spoke to her in Spanish. Before Mr. Dennis could finish translating to her what Lynn had told him, Mrs. Dennis sprang from her chair, clasped her hands together as if she were praying, and began wailing.

"*Mi hijo! Mi hijo! Dónde está mi hijo! Mi Dios! Mi Dios!*"

Lynn needed no translation. He could recognize a parent's distress in any language. As Mrs. Dennis continued to cry and mumble in Spanish, Mr. Dennis bolted from the room, and Lynn could hear the pounding of his footsteps racing up the stairs to the second floor. Within a few seconds, he was back in the living room holding an empty shoe box. The minute Mrs. Dennis saw it, her wailing escalated into shrills.

"No! No! *Mi hijo! Por qué?*"

"This is the shoe box where I keep my gun," Mr. Dennis explained to Lynn as he pulled his hysterical wife to him and she buried her face in his chest. Mr. Dennis' face showed a combination of fear and helplessness that he could not camouflage. He tried to muffle the sound of his wife's screams with his chest, so that the other children wouldn't hear the terror that was occurring in the living room of their otherwise peaceful home.

Lynn pulled out his cell phone and punched his speed-dial number for the police. In his line of business, he had to work with the police often regarding reports of child abuse, truancy, potential suicides—the list of issues went on and on. The dispatcher immediately connected Lynn with one of the police sergeants and Lynn explained the situation to him. After he hung up the phone, he informed Mr. Dennis that the police would be arriving at the house momentarily. With his wife's face still buried in his chest, Mr. Dennis picked up the phone.

"Dayton has a part-time job that he works a few hours after school and on weekends at a grocery store a few blocks from here. I'm calling to see if he's there," Mr. Dennis announced to no one in particular. After a few seconds, Lynn heard Mr. Dennis asking to speak with his son. He watched as Mr. Dennis' face went pale and he hung up the phone.

"Dayton didn't show up for work, and no one at the store has seen or heard from him since yesterday." He stumbled through the words, barely able to get them out. It was if they were too heavy in his mouth and made it difficult for him to speak.

"Well, I understand that your son was at school today. He met with his guidance counselor. So at least we have that," said Lynn.

They stood in awkward silence for a few minutes until they heard a knock at the door. Mr. Dennis guided his wife to the sofa and helped her sit down. Her earlier outbursts seemed to have drained her of energy, and she silently collapsed on the sofa, the glow from the candles highlighting the tears streaming down her face. Mr. Dennis opened the front door and was relieved to see two police officers standing on his porch. He was surprised that they had arrived so quickly, as police response to calls in his neighborhood typically took at least twenty minutes.

In fact, that's why Joseph Dennis had purchased the gun in the first place. There had been quite a few break-ins in the neighborhood lately and he had gotten the gun to protect his family. Aside from his wife, Dayton was the only other member of the family whom he had told about the gun in case something happened when he was not home. Up until recently, Mr. Dennis had worked as a New York Transit bus driver. A few months ago, he had lost his job due to budget cuts and was working part time delivering newspapers and driving a gypsy cab while he looked for a full-time job. Before losing his job altogether, his hours had been drastically cut, making it impossible for him to keep up with all the family's bills, even resulting in their electricity being disconnected.

With a wife who didn't work outside the home and five children to support, Mr. Dennis was having a difficult time keeping his family afloat. Without Dayton's part-time job to help out, they would not be able to put food on the table. As it was, they ate mostly staple foods like rice and beans and flour tortillas that Rosa made by hand to save money. On top of that, their youngest child, four-year old Lena, had bouts with asthma, and frequent trips to the doctor had pushed the family's finances far into the red.

"We were in the neighborhood and got a call from dispatch to this address," said one of the police officers as they followed Mr. Dennis into the living room.

Lynn approached the officers and immediately identified himself as an investigator with the Bureau of Child Welfare. He explained to them the sequence of events that had brought him to the Dennis home that evening and the reason for the call to the police. After hearing all the facts, the officers began to question the Dennises about their son's whereabouts. Fortunately, one of the police officers was fluent in Spanish and was able to speak directly to Mrs. Dennis in her first language. Being able to converse with the police without having to wait for her husband to translate seemed to help Mrs. Dennis calm down a bit.

"Can you give me the names and addresses of any friends that your son might be with?" asked one of the police officers.

"With school and working in the evenings and on the weekends, Dayton doesn't have a lot of time to do much hanging out with friends," Mr. Dennis replied. "In the evenings after work at the grocery store, he comes home to do his schoolwork and to help the younger kids with their homework and help his mother get them to bed," Mr. Dennis continued. He shook his head. If Dayton wasn't at the grocery store, they had no idea where he could be. He gave the police the name of one classmate that Dayton had grown up with in the neighborhood and whom he occasionally got together with to shoot a few hoops, but other than that, they were pretty certain that Dayton didn't have many friends.

The police officers got all the information they could from Lynn and the Dennises, then stood to leave. They assured Mr. and Mrs. Dennis that they would do all they could to find their son and asked them to please call if they heard from Dayton. After the officers left, Rosa Dennis continued to sit perched in her spot on the sofa. Lynn could tell that she was far away, adrift on an island of despair, longing for the safe return of her eldest son.

At this point, there was nothing left for Lynn to do. Now, it was a matter of waiting—waiting to hear from the police or to see if Dayton came home. Lynn explained to Mr. Dennis that if Dayton returned home, his parents were required to take him for a psychiatric evaluation before he could return to school. He provided Mr. Dennis with a written sheet of instructions telling him where to take his son and what type of documentation the school would need before he would be allowed back.

"Thank you for your help," said Mr. Dennis as he walked Lynn to the door.

"Here's my card," said Lynn. "If you hear anything tonight, give me a call. Otherwise, I'll call you tomorrow morning." He shook Mr. Dennis' hand and stepped out into the cold night air. As he walked the two blocks to his car, he felt an overwhelming urge to get home to his wife and boys.

chapter 9

Dayton

DAYTON HATED BEING THE OLDEST of his siblings. That meant that he was the one his parents counted on for everything. Since his dad had to be up and out on his paper route very early each morning, Dayton was the one who helped his mother get the younger kids ready for school before getting to school himself. He was the one his parents expected to set an example for his younger siblings by getting good grades in school so that he could go to college. When his dad lost his job a few months ago, Dayton felt like he had no choice but to get a part-time job to help his family make ends meet.

He knew that although his parents hadn't said anything to him about it, they were counting on him to help them get through the tough times that had hit his family and hit them hard. Since his dad lost his job, Dayton's part-time income had become a major source of the family's finances. In fact, he had given his parents the money he had saved from working summer jobs over the last several years so they could pay up the mortgage on the house, which had fallen three months behind. His dad didn't want to take the money, but Dayton knew that without it, his family would lose their home. What would happen to them then? So he had insisted even though it had taken every penny of his savings. Dayton could see the pain in his dad's face when he finally accepted the offer of the funds. His dad had promised to pay him back once he got on his feet again.

Over the last few months, Dayton found it harder and harder to get through his routine: getting up early in the morning to help his mother get the younger kids' breakfast and get them ready for school; putting in a full day of school himself and then heading straight to his job at the grocery store; getting home to help his siblings with homework and afterwards, doing whatever schoolwork he had to get done for himself. In the midst of it all, the resounding silence from Harvard hung over his head like a looming black cloud.

Dayton was tired. He felt overwhelmed with his life. A few days ago when the electricity was disconnected, he had realized just how bad off the situation at home had become. To make matters worse, he hadn't gotten into Harvard, his dream school. He certainly would have heard from them by now if the news had been good. Now it was too late to apply anywhere else. Surely he had ruined his life by applying to just one school.

He couldn't take it anymore. After a sleepless night of staring at the ceiling in his bedroom, he decided that he would put an end to it all. So he had written a goodbye note to Mr. Carlton, who was his favorite person at Thurman. He had gotten to school extra early before any of the staff had arrived, slipped the unsigned note under Mr. Carlton's door, and gone to his classes as usual.

But before he had even left for school, Dayton had removed his father's gun from its hiding place in the shoe box on the top shelf of his parents' bedroom closet and packed it in his book bag. Unlike many of the other schools in the Bronx, Thurman had not installed a metal scanner, nor were students subjected to pat downs when entering the premises. He planned to wait until after school and go to his special place in the park not far from where he lived. He often went there to sort out his thoughts, or sometimes to study if it got too noisy at home.

Dayton thought it was ironic that he walked around at school all day carrying a weapon of destruction in his innocent-looking book bag. He grew concerned when we was called to Mr. Carlton's office, thinking that the counselor had figured out that he was the one who left the note under his door. When he met with Mr. Carlton, though, he just wanted to know if Dayton had discussed his college options with his parents and routine stuff about his going away to school. Dayton liked Mr. Carlton, and felt that he was genuinely interested in the success of his students. When their meeting was over and Dayton stood to leave, for a brief moment he thought about talking to Mr. Carlton about the problems he was having at home and his thoughts of suicide. Then Mr. Carlton's phone rang, and as quickly as the thought had entered his head, it had disappeared, and Dayton was on his way out of Mr. Carlton's office and back down the corridor, back to class, and back on track with his plan.

The school day dragged by for Dayton; each minute seemed like an hour. Finally the bell rang, signifying the end of classes, and Dayton headed for the park. He would wait in the park until it got dark. He figured that with the weather being so cold, the park would be relatively empty. Besides, it was a small park which took up only a few city blocks, was mostly concrete, and had little to offer in the way of beauty and ambiance. Most people used it simply as a shortcut on their way to and from the bus stop or the local bodegas.

Dayton had been sitting in the park for hours now, in the cold, his book bag in his lap. Scenes from home played through his head like an old movie— his mom stirring a pot of rice and beans on the stove for dinner; his siblings sitting around the kitchen table doing homework; his dad surfing the advertisement section of the newspaper looking for work. Normally, Dayton would be getting home from his job at the store about this time in the evening. As he sat in the park just a few short blocks from home, he doubted that anyone would even notice when he didn't arrive home at his regular time tonight. He doubted that any of his classmates would shed even one tear tomorrow when they learned of his death. He felt insignificant. His life didn't matter to anyone—not even to him.

As he gave the park one last perusal and saw that there was no one there but him, he slowly took the gun out of his book bag. For the entire time he had been sitting in the park, he hadn't noticed the cold. He hadn't been cold at all. In fact, his face and hands were sweaty and hot. But as he took the gun out of his book bag, it felt like a piece of ice in his hands. For a moment, he was stunned by how cold and heavy the piece of metal that he had been carrying around all day felt as he held it in his palm. Before another thought could enter his head, Dayton quickly placed the gun in his mouth and pulled the trigger.

Then, there was total darkness.

chapter 10

THE RESTAURANT WAS FAIRLY CROWDED when Lois and Miki finally took seats at a table near a big picture window that looked out onto 2nd Avenue. Lois let out a big sigh as she sat down in her seat. She felt far away from the problems that had plagued her day. It felt good to take a little time to enjoy herself and to visit with her best friend.

"So, how have you been?" asked Miki as she took a sip from the glass of wine she had ordered.

"I'm fine," Lois responded. "You know how it is at my school—always some fires to put out, and today was no different. How about you? How are things at work?" Just as Lois finished her question, the cup of tea she ordered arrived along with a bowl containing several lemon slices. Lois didn't drink alcohol. It was a vow she had taken back when she and Miki were college roommates. One night, Miki had come home in tears after seeing her boyfriend cuddled up in a corner of the student lounge with another girl. Lois had broken up with her boyfriend a few weeks earlier after he told her he was gay. That night Miki and Lois had decided to drown their sorrows in more than a few bottles of wine.

They had pooled their coins together, gone to the liquor store, and come back with several of the cheapest bottles of wine that money could buy. Until this day, all that Lois could remember about the wine was that it was named after a bird—Cold Duck or Wild Turkey or something to that effect. Anyway, she and Miki had spent that night gulping wine and singing the "I Ain't Got No Man" blues until they passed out or fell asleep; the details were still unclear to Lois. The next day, Lois had awakened running to the bathroom, and that's where she stayed for the next three days. The smell of cheap wine seeped from every pore of her skin. She felt sicker than she had ever been in her life. For days, she couldn't keep anything in her stomach, not even water. She remembered praying to God that if he would just let her survive, she would never take another drink for as long as she lived. Now, a woman in her fifties, it was a vow that Lois had never broken and one about which she had never had any regrets. Till this day, even the smell of wine made her stomach a little queasy.

"All is well at work," said Miki. "Nothing much has changed. I did get a new assistant and I think she's going to work out fine once she learns her way around. I see the vow is still intact," she said, smiling as Lois took a sip of her tea.

They both laughed as they often did when they reminisced about that night. Both Lois and Miki loved it when they got together. They enjoyed talking about old times and for a brief moment, they were both those young, wide-eyed girls again, their futures blank canvases before them, full of dreams and possibilities. Each time they met for dinner, they always hurried to get the small talk about their jobs out of the way before spending the rest of the time reminiscing about their college days and updating each other about old college acquaintances they may have seen or heard from. Tonight was no different. They spent the next two hours talking about old friends and exchanging stories about the past.

After they finished their dinner, they both ordered dessert and coffee. While they chatted and enjoyed their dessert, Lois could feel that someone was watching her. She looked out the restaurant window directly into the face of the homeless woman she had passed near the subway on her way to the restaurant. Miki, who had been chatting away, finally noticed that Lois was staring out the window and looked to see what had caught her attention. She was a bit startled when her eyes landed on those of the homeless woman, whose face, with the street light glaring behind her, looked tired and weathered and whose eyes were clouded like those of a person who had seen too much.

"I don't know why the city doesn't do something about these homeless people," said Miki. "It seems like they're just getting out of hand. Why isn't this woman in a shelter instead of on the street? Beneath all the dirt and grime, she appears to be a pretty nice-looking woman. Why doesn't she just get a job and take care of herself?"

Something about Miki's comment took Lois back to when she was in grade school, back in Tennessee. Lois flashed back to her humble beginnings. All the families she knew had been poor when she was growing up, including her own. Specifically, she remembered her friend Dora Simon. Lois had known Dora all of her life. Their mothers had known each other since they themselves were girls and had remained good friends after becoming adults and having families of their own. Lois' mother and Dora's mother both had large families—eight and seven children, respectively. Lois and Dora had grown up like sisters, always at each other's house, and each respective mother treated each like her own daughter. Dora was only nine months older than Lois, and they attended the same grade school, junior high school, and high school.

"You know, Miki, pardon the cliché, but you shouldn't judge a person until you've walked in their shoes," Lois replied to Miki's comments about the homeless woman. "When I was in grade school," she continued, "I had a friend, Dora, who used to come to school from time to time wearing two left shoes, hoping I'm sure that none of us kids would notice. Of course, we did notice and my friend often became the butt of unceasing teasing and ridicule. I remember how badly I felt for her when the other kids would pick on her, but I didn't know what to do to help her. I remember thinking that Dora had brought the ridicule on herself by choosing to wear two left shoes to school. It wasn't until long after grade school when she and I were reminiscing one day about those times, that I finally asked her why she would come to school wearing two left shoes.

"Dora explained to me that her mom worked as a housekeeper for a woman who had only one leg. This woman always bought the same style and color shoes, and since she could only use one of a pair she would give its mate to Dora's mom. Dora had been lucky enough, or unlucky enough, as the case may be, to have the same size foot as her mom's employer. Since there wasn't much money in either of our families for new shoes back in those days, her mom would make her wear two of the leftover left shoes to school.

"After I learned this, I promised myself that I would never judge anyone else without first knowing their circumstances. Dora and I are friends to this day. That same girl who wore two left shoes to school now owns her own company and travels the world giving business lectures and seminars. We can laugh about it now, but in those days our parents simply did what they had to do to survive and take care of their families. I always joke with Dora now that those two left shoes from her childhood had kept her pointed in the right direction—forward."

"I'm sorry," said Miki after Lois had finished her story. "You are absolutely right about not forming blind opinions about other people. We don't know how this woman came to be homeless, and these days with the economy the way it is, it's easier than we might think."

"Exactly," Lois responded, smiling at Miki. That was one of the qualities that she loved most about Miki. She was always the first to acknowledge her mistakes and try to learn from them.

"I wish there was something we could do for this woman," Miki replied.

"I know how you feel," said Lois. "That's why I work at the community shelter every other Sunday teaching people how to read and write. There are thousands of people just like her in this city alone. Unfortunately, you can't help them all."

"No, I can't. But I can start by giving this woman the rest of my dessert. Let me have yours too," Miki said as she reached over and took Lois' dessert plate that held half a piece of cherry pie. "She looks like she could use something to eat. The others I'll pray for."

While Miki asked their waiter for a leftover box for the dessert, Lois left her portion of the bill and went to retrieve their coats from the coat check area. It felt good to have spent some time with her old friend and to see that neither of them had lost their desire to do good things for others. As she waited for Miki to join her at the front door, she was happy that she had braved the cold and met her friend for dinner.

Stepping out of the restaurant into the damp air, Lois felt a sense of rejuvenation as she flagged a cab to take her home. She couldn't wait to get home, throw on her pj's, and snuggle on the living room sofa beside her husband, Reuben—the perfect ending to a long day.

chapter 11

DAYTON DENNIS SLOWLY OPENED HIS eyes. He was in a daze. Where am I? Am I dead? He thought back to the gun and saw himself pulling the trigger. I must be dead. Then suddenly, he felt his heart pounding rapidly inside his chest. After a few minutes of struggling to get his bearings, he realized that he was lying facedown on the ground in front of the bench where he had been sitting. He felt the hardness of his father's revolver poking beneath his chest. Dayton slowly sat up and took the gun in his frozen fingers. What happened? Why hadn't it fired? His mind struggled to pull the pieces together. He opened the cylinder of the revolver and to his surprise saw that each cartridge chamber was empty.

In his haste to grab the gun from its hiding place in his parents' bedroom without being seen by anyone, Dayton had forgotten to grab the box of cartridges his father kept hidden in back of his sock drawer. He remembered his father explaining to him when he had brought the gun home that because of the other kids in the house, he didn't want to keep it loaded or keep the bullets and the gun in the same place. After placing the gun in his mouth and pulling the trigger, Dayton realized that he must have passed out. He had botched his suicide. He was very much alive. Suddenly, he felt tired and cold. He stumbled to his feet and looked around to see if anyone had seen him and wondered how long he had been unconscious.

The park was still empty. If anyone had seen him while he was sprawled on the ground, they probably thought he was passed out drunk, or homeless—not an unusual scene for anyone living in New York. He grabbed his wool gloves from the pocket of his jacket and pulled them over his numb fingers. He looked around for his backpack, but it was nowhere to be found. Suddenly, he noticed the pungent smell of urine emanating from his jacket. Someone had stolen his backpack and pissed on him while he was unconscious on the ground. Sliding his hand into the back pocket of his jeans, he discovered that the ten dollars he had placed there was gone.

"Son of a bitch!" Dayton was startled by the sound of his own voice uttering profanities.

"I can't believe that somebody stole my damn backpack, my last ten dollars, and then pissed on me!" Without waiting for his brain to put it all together, Dayton stuffed the gun into the deep pocket of his jacket and started the few blocks home.

As he walked, he suddenly became aware of the pungent taste of metal on his tongue, which, along with the smell of urine from his jacket, served as lingering reminders of the foiled task he had yet to execute. I'll try again tomorrow, he thought as he cut through the park and turned the corner onto his street.

Within a few minutes, Dayton was standing on his front porch. He was sure his father hadn't noticed that the gun was missing from its hiding place in the closet. He hadn't seen his father with the gun since the day he bought it. Maybe it was because of the other kids in the house, but whatever the reason, his father never took the gun out of the shoe box. Mr. Dennis was not a gun fanatic and had purchased the weapon only to protect his family in case of a break-in. Otherwise, he acted as if it didn't exist.

Dayton opened the front door and stepped into the foyer. Immediately, he could feel that something was wrong. Before he could gather his thoughts, his parents emerged from the living room. His mother quickly ran to him and hugged him so tightly that Dayton found it hard to catch his breath. "*Mi hijo! Mi hijo,*" Rosa mumbled, clinging to her son, undeterred by the strong stench of urine coming from the sleeve of his jacket.

"What's going on? What's wrong with Mom?" Dayton turned to his dad in bewilderment.

With his mother still clinging to him, Mr. Dennis led them into the living room and shut the door. He motioned for Dayton to take a seat on the sofa. Mrs. Dennis sat beside her son, tears streaming down her face. Joseph Dennis took a deep breath and began to speak in a slow, serious tone.

"Son, a caseworker just left here a short while ago. Someone at your school found a suicide note and they say you wrote it." Mr. Dennis reached down and picked up the empty shoe box beside the sofa and showed it to Dayton. "Other than Rosa and me, you are the only one who knew I even had a gun and where I kept it," Mr. Dennis continued.

Dayton could feel his heart sink and slide down into his shoes. He had never seen his parents so upset, not even when his father lost his job or when their electricity was turned off. Although his father continued talking to him and Dayton could see his mouth moving, he couldn't hear what he was saying. For a few moments, he felt like none of it was real. He felt like he was watching a movie on TV with the sound turned down. Then he heard his father ask him for the gun, and it triggered his brain to start working again and he was back with his parents in their living room. He realized that the horrible scene that was playing through his head was really happening. His parents knew about his plans to commit suicide.

Not only did they know, but look at what it has done to them, Dayton thought, and for a moment, he was concerned that he had spoken his thought out loud. The effect that his death might have on his family was something that Dayton had not considered when he made his suicide plans. Although his dad was typically guarded with his emotions, he could see how this was affecting him to the core. Seeing his father choking back the lump in his throat and holding back the tears in the corner of his eyes as he spoke, Dayton knew he was in a great deal of pain—pain that he had caused. His mother was beyond upset, clinging to Dayton and sobbing helplessly. Dayton slowly stood up, reached into his pocket, took out the gun, and handed it to his father.

Taking the gun in his hands, Joseph Dennis could no longer contain himself. Tears began to rush down the side of his face. He grabbed his son and hugged him so tightly that he couldn't distinguish the beat of his own heart from that of his son's. Finally, Mr. Dennis stepped back, dried his face on his handkerchief, and picked up the phone, and dialed Lynn Marshall, the caseworker. After a few minutes, he hung up the phone.

"Dayton, I have to take you to the hospital for evaluation. We have to go now," Mr. Dennis announced. "The caseworker says that you won't be able to go back to school until you have been seen by a psychiatrist and the psychiatrist says that it's okay for you to return." The words sat so heavily on his tongue that he had trouble getting them out.

Dayton followed his father out of the living room, into the foyer, and out the door to the car. Sitting beside his dad in the car as they maneuvered corners and sat waiting for red lights to turn green, Dayton became nauseous. He wasn't sure if it was because he hadn't eaten at all during the course of the day, but suddenly he felt light-headed and everything seemed to be swirling around him. His world was spinning out of control. Only a few hours ago, he had everything planned. He knew how to solve his problems. One shot and his misery would have been over. Now, all of these people had intruded on his plan. Mr. Carlton, the state caseworker, his parents—they all knew his secret. Yes, Dayton had written the letter and left it in Mr. Carlton's office, but he had imagined that by the time Mr. Carlton figured out who had left it, it would be too late for him to interfere.

Leaning his head back on the headrest of his seat, Dayton shut his eyes and tried to swallow the vile taste that bubbled up from his stomach into his throat. Even with his eyes closed, he could still see the simultaneous look of terror and relief on his mother's face and the pain in his father's eyes when he had arrived home just minutes earlier.

What have I done? How could I have hurt my parents like that? Will they ever be able to forgive me? Will I ever be able to forgive myself? Questions flowed in and out of Dayton's head so fast that he couldn't quite grasp them all. Along with these questions, one question hung in the air around him, making the air in the car thick and unbreathable. Am I still able to execute my plan even though I know what grief it will cause my family? So many questions plagued Dayton's brain that he was in a dazed state of confusion when their car finally pulled into the parking lot at Jacoby Hospital. Inside the building, walking beside his dad down the long, main corridor, he couldn't help but feel anxious about where this path might lead him.

chapter 12

Mia

SLEET WAS COMING DOWN HARD outside Mia's window as she climbed out of bed and headed for the bathroom to get dressed for school. Her three-day suspension was over and she was looking forward to erasing her boredom by going through the motions of a high school student. She missed cutting class with Lily to grab a smoke outside. She also missed making her teachers' lives miserable with every opportunity that presented itself, especially Mr. Carlton's. Suddenly, she remembered that she had a score to settle with him. He had told Ms. Drake about seeing her in the hall when she was supposed to be in class and about her cursing at him that day in his office. Because of Mr. Carlton, Mia had gotten a three-day suspension instead of Ms. Drake's usual two days.

"Wait till I see him again," Mia said under her breath. "I'm going to curse his ass out good."

Mia was glad that her mother had already left for work. She was a nurse's aide at a long-term care facility on Manhattan's West Side and worked a lot of overtime hours so that she could provide Mia with whatever she wanted. Mia's mother babied and spoiled her. Whenever Mia got into trouble at school, her mother always took Mia's side. She had even made several trips to the school to complain to the principal about how the teachers mistreated her golden child. Mia knew she had her mother bamboozled. Whatever Mia told her mother, she believed.

Sometimes, when her mother didn't have to be at work so early, she would walk with Mia to the subway station, rattling on to her about some craziness that was going on at her job. Mia hated it when her mother walked to the subway with her because that meant she wouldn't be able to "crack an egg" on her way to school. That's what she and Lily called their method of picking up extra spending money. They would spot an old woman, unlucky enough to be on the street that particular morning, and one of them would run up behind the woman to startle her while the other one snatched her purse. They had done it more times than Mia could remember and had managed never to have gotten caught.

Mia didn't really need the money they took. Her mother always gave her a ten-dollar bill each day before she left for work—a fifty dollar per week allowance. Mia cracked eggs just for the fun of it. She loved to see the terror on the old women's faces, some of them turning various shades of red as their eyes bulged in shock and panic. Mostly, they picked up a few dollars, but every so often, they would luck out and get a woman who might have been on her way to the bank to make a deposit and end up with a nice little bundle. Once they had ended up with over three hundred dollars, which they split between them. Mia had spent most of her half on CDs, boxes of cigarettes, and nail polish.

Although the sleet had stopped by the time Mia stepped outside her apartment building and headed for school, the brisk air caused her to pull up the collar of her down jacket. She was looking forward to getting back into her daily routine of being a pain in the neck to her teachers and hanging out with Lily. As she walked the long block that led to the subway, she spotted a frail-looking old woman slowly edging her way down the sidewalk across the street from her. She carried a small, black purse which hung loosely from her wrist, and with her other hand she clutched the top of her coat to block out the cold air.

"An egg! This will be an easy one to crack," Mia said out loud as she slowed her pace and crossed the street. Although Mia had never cracked an egg without Lily before, this one seemed like it was perfect for just one person to manage. Just as Mia neared the woman from behind, suddenly the woman slipped on the wet sidewalk. Her feet flew up in the air and she landed hard on her side on the pavement. Mia heard a loud crack as the old woman's body met with the hard concrete. Her purse landed a few feet away. In a split second, Mia quickly ran to where the purse had landed, scooped it up, and continued running until she reached the subway station.

She couldn't wait to tell Lily how funny the old lady looked flying up in the air and landing in a heap on the concrete. She and Lily would have a good laugh as they often did after cracking eggs. As the subway train got closer to Mia's stop for school, she grew more excited and anxious about telling Lily about her morning adventure. When the train came to her stop, Mia rushed up the stairs leading from the subway platform to the street. She hurriedly walked the half-block to school, still clutching the old woman's purse in her hand. She would wait until she met with Lily during their homeroom class and they would go through the purse together.

chapter 13

Lily

LILY HAD BARELY STEPPED OUT onto her front porch when she heard the phone ringing inside the house. Her father, who was a night security guard at one of the big office buildings in Manhattan, hadn't gotten home from work yet. She was looking forward to her day at school, because Mia would be back from her suspension today.

Lily lived with her father and paternal grandmother, both of whom she adored. They lived in the Bronx in the house that her father had grown up in. Her grandfather, who died when her father was a boy, had bought the house with money he saved working for years as a Pullman car porter. Her grandmother, whom Lily called "Nanna," had been telling Lily stories about her grandfather as far back as she could remember. Nanna had told Lily countless times how her grandfather's life had tragically ended when the train he was working that day jumped a rail, killing several people on board. Although it was a sad story, Nanna always ended by saying that she was glad her husband had died doing what he enjoyed—riding the train.

Lily had never met her mother. When her father was a young man in his twenties, he had had a one-night stand with a young woman he met in a bar. They had spent the night in the back seat of his car. Although they had exchanged phone numbers, neither of them for whatever reason had called the other, until about a year later when her father received a call from the woman, who asked for his address. The next evening, the doorbell rang, and when her father opened the door, sitting on the porch was a plastic laundry basket containing a sleeping baby, a birth certificate, and a short note:

This is your daughter.

I named her Lily after my favorite flower.

Please take care of her.

Nanna and Lily's father had searched for Lily's mother for a long time after that, to no avail. She had given a false name at the hospital when Lily was born and on Lily's birth certificate. To complicate matters even more, the one night Lily's parents had spent together, they had exchanged only first names.

All Lily knew about her mother was that her first name was Carol. Sometimes, when Lily walked down the street, she would catch herself staring curiously at women she passed, and a small part of her deep inside wondered, are you my mother? Whenever she encountered a waitress, the lady behind the counter at the drugstore, or any other woman wearing a name tag that read "Carol," Lily was always careful to treat her extra nice.

Lily dropped her book bag on the front porch and ran back to the door to go in and answer the phone. Nanna had left the house early, as she did three days out of the week, for the senior citizen center to visit her friends there. They would spend the day playing bingo, listening to opera music, and chatting about the days when they were young and life was good. Although the center was only four blocks away, Nanna always called a cab to take her since arthritis in her legs made it difficult for her to walk even short distances. On days that she went to the center, Nanna always woke Lily to get up for school and would leave breakfast on the stove for her.

The phone rang several more times before Lily got the front door unlocked and ran back inside. She hoped she could reach it before it stopped ringing. Maybe it was her father calling to ask her to stop to pick up his work shirts from the laundry on her way home from school. Lily picked up the receiver and before she could say anything, she heard a woman's high-pitched voice on the other end. It was their neighbor, Mrs. Munchie, and she was hysterical.

It took Lily a few minutes to understand what Mrs. Munchie was trying to tell her. Suddenly, she slammed the receiver back on the phone and ran out the door down the street. As she ran, Lily could hear her heart throbbing so loudly she was sure that everyone she passed could hear its deafening banging inside her chest. But she didn't care. All she cared about was getting to her destination—that one little spot on earth where her whole world had just came crashing down.

chapter 14

Mr. Carlton

MR. CARLTON HAD ARRIVED AT his office just seconds before the first period class bell rang (unusually late for him). He felt drained. He stared again at the letter in his hand from the school district in response to his application for a principal position.

Dear Mr. Carlton:

Thank you for your interest in becoming a principal in our district. There were many qualified applicants for the position and we have selected an outstanding candidate whom we feel is well suited for the role.

Best wishes for your continued success.

He had known what the letter said before he even opened it. He had gotten many of these letters over the years and they all said the same thing—thanks, but no thanks. Each time he received a rejection letter, he became angry and annoyed, more so with himself than with anyone else. He couldn't understand why he kept trying after so many no's.

His mind often drifted back to when he was a young man, fresh out of grad school, and chose to forego the business world for an opportunity to work as a teacher in the New York City school system. If his legs were long enough, he'd swing them around and kick himself in the seat of his pants!

What was he thinking choosing a profession where the pay and appreciation was minuscule, but the work grueling? Had he gone into a different field, he could have been a lot better off financially. Maybe even well enough off to afford one of those swanky apartments over on the East Side instead of his six-story walk-up downtown. After all, that's why his wife, Nona, had left him. She wanted some of the finer things in life that a teacher's salary simply couldn't provide.

One day, arriving home to his beautiful wife of more than three years, Mr. Carlton found only an empty apartment. It was empty in every sense of the word. Nona had taken everything, even the curtains from the windows. The apartment had been stripped clean of everything that would have even hinted that two people in love had shared a home there. All that was left were his clothes hanging in the closet, which provided the only indication for him that he was in the right apartment. Not only had Nona taken every physical object in sight, but it seemed that she had stripped the place of even the memory of her having ever lived there.

The scent of her Chanel perfume that usually wafted in the air of the small apartment and was the first to greet anyone who opened the front door—gone.

The big bowl of fresh, green apples that she kept on the coffee table because they matched the color of the living room wall—gone.

The softness of her arms around his neck as she welcomed him home from his long day, and the sound of her chattering on about the gourmet dessert she had prepared for his dinner—all gone.

What had working in the education field done for him? It had caused him to lose everything, including the only woman he'd ever loved. If only he could go back in time and make some different choices.

After Nona left him, Mr. Carlton began to despise his career. Over the years, he had moved to and from more schools than he could count, trying to find something that would ignite that old fire he once had about teaching. He had taught in the classroom for many years, and then decided that he might be better off if he became a guidance counselor. Now, after many years as a counselor, he thought that maybe if he got into the administrative side of education and became a principal, he would rediscover the passion he once had for a career in education. So he acquired a principal's license and continued to apply for principal positions, hoping that eventually his number would come up, but so far it hadn't.

Every day he came to work hoping that something would trigger in him the excitement he once had for his job, but every day he left disappointed. Even the incident that happened with Dayton Dennis hadn't erupted within him a satisfaction that was sustainable for more than just a few days. He was happy that Dayton's suicide plans had been discovered before he was able to execute them. But, after the adrenaline wore off, Mr. Carlton found himself back in his humdrum state of mind.

Day after day, he forced himself to get out of bed, get dressed, and go to work. Day after day, he held meaningless conversations with his students, their parents, and his co-workers. Day after day, he came home to his empty apartment. Although several years had passed since Nona left and he had refurnished his place, to him it was still as empty as the day he came home and found her gone. So aside from the time he spent at work, he spent most of his time sitting in his small apartment, hoping—praying—begging—that one day he would find what he needed to fill the emptiness that Nona had left behind.

chapter 15

When Lois Met Reuben

THANKFUL THAT THE DAY HAD gotten off to a quiet start, Lois Roberts sat behind the desk in her office. She had already completed her morning walk through the corridors of Thurman High School and was sipping from her cup of tea when she heard the phone ring in her outer office. Within a few seconds her assistant, Sylvia, called to her that her husband was on the line. Lois immediately breathed a sigh of relief. She was glad it wasn't someone calling with a problem. She needed a few minutes of peace before stepping into her busy day. She was so grateful that it was Reuben on the phone. Besides, when she woke up this morning, Reuben had already left the house for work. He was an editor at a large publishing company downtown and liked to get to work even earlier than Lois. She was glad to have an opportunity to speak to him before starting her day.

After talking to Reuben, Lois felt energized. Even after many years of marriage, Reuben still had that effect on her. The sound of his voice, the touch of his hand still made her feel complete. Her mind drifted back to the first time they met.

She had been living in New York for about ten years at that time and was settling into a new apartment in Queens. She had started a new job a few weeks earlier and was walking from her apartment to the subway station to catch the train to Manhattan to work. She had overslept that morning and was walking quite briskly trying to make up some time. Suddenly, she noticed a man walking just in front of her, heading in the same direction. When they arrived at the corner, the traffic light turned red and she found herself standing beside this man while they waited for the light to change. After a few seconds of watching the light, the man turned and spoke to her. His voice sounded as profound and opulent as he looked and Lois was immediately intrigued by him.

"It's a nice day, isn't it?"

"Yes it is," Lois replied. Just then, the light changed and she started across the street with the man walking a few steps behind her.

Lois hadn't dated much during the time she had been in New York. With completing her undergraduate degree, then years of graduate school, all while holding whatever job she could find to support herself, there wasn't much time left for dating. Besides, Lois wasn't into recreational dating—she was looking for the person to spend the rest of her life with. The few dates she had had over the years she had scared off by asking them right upfront their views on marriage, having children, women having careers, and similar topics that most men felt were much too serious for initial conversations. Lois didn't care. She didn't want to waste time dating someone only to find out later that he had no interest in getting married. So she always laid her cards on the table right away.

As she walked past this man on the corner that morning, Lois felt an uncontrollable desire to know more about him. Tugging at the sleeve of her blouse to cover her watch, she turned and spoke again to the man.

"Excuse me, do you have the time?"

After he told her the time, he and Lois ended up walking to the subway station together and standing together on the train as they headed for downtown. She learned that his name was Reuben Russell, that he was born and raised in Manhattan, but had lived in Washington, D.C., for several years before moving back to New York only a few weeks earlier. They chatted the whole way into Manhattan, and just before the train reached his stop, he asked Lois for her work number and suggested that he would call her sometime and meet her for lunch. When he opened his briefcase to retrieve a pen and paper to take her number, Lois noticed a small bible among his papers.

This guy is either one of those religious fanatics who's going to be constantly preaching at me and trying to convert me to whatever it is that he's into or he's just a nice guy who tries to live his life by the golden rule, she thought. Lois was delighted when it turned out to be the latter. She and Reuben began dating and were married a few years later. Lois couldn't believe that this year they would be celebrating their twenty-fifth wedding anniversary. The years had passed by so quickly.

The sound of her phone ringing again brought Lois back from the past, but she brought back with her a warm feeling inside. Although she couldn't tell if it was the hot tea or the warm memories that had caused the surge of heat within her, she was comforted by it. She knew she had a lot in her life to be thankful for, and the man that God had sent to her on a crowded street corner in New York so many years ago was at the top of her list.

"Tell them I'm on my way," she called out to Sylvia as she left her office and headed down the hallway to her first meeting of the day.

chapter 16

Mia WAS DISAPPOINTED WHEN SHE arrived at school and found that Lily was not there. She asked around, but none of the other kids had seen her. Where was she? Didn't Lily know that today was her day back from suspension? Other than Lily, Mia had no one to talk to. She hated the other girls in her freshman class. They were always tattling on her for one thing or the other and were big babies as far as Mia was concerned. Maybe Lily will show up by next period, Mia thought hopefully as she took her seat in the back row near the window.

As she placed her book bag down on her desk, she realized that she was still holding the old woman's purse in her hand. She quickly opened her book bag and shoved the purse inside. If Lily didn't show up by lunch period, she would go through the purse by herself and Lily would miss out on the fun.

"Serves her right for not being here," Mia sighed, sliding down in her seat and propping her feet on the desk in front of her. It was going to be a long day without Lily to laugh and talk with. Even being mean to the other girls wouldn't be any fun without Lily.

By second period, there was still no sign of Lily. Mia sat fidgeting at her desk as she waited for Ms. Brown to arrive. Great, Mia thought. Not only do I have this woman for homeroom, I'm lucky enough to have her for history too! Her thoughts were interrupted as Ms. Brown walked in and shouted for everyone to take their seats and take out their history books. Mia hated history and she especially hated having it with Ms. Brown, who talked endlessly about ancient people and events. She couldn't see how something that happened hundreds of years ago could help her now. History was boring and useless, a sentiment she held for all of her courses. Besides, the only thing she wanted to know about dead presidents was how many she had in her wallet.

Mia was glad when the bell signifying the end of the period finally rang. It seemed as if she had been sitting for an eternity, listening to Ms. Brown go on and on about some ancient, uninteresting event that no one cared about except Ms. Brown.

Time to sneak outside and have a smoke, she thought as she stepped from the classroom into the hallway. She really needed a cigarette.

While the hallway crowded up with students going to exchange books from their lockers and heading to their next class, Mia slipped out the exit door. Although the air outside was still cold and damp, it felt good to get out of the building. Reaching into her book bag for her cigarettes, her fingers reminded her of the old woman's purse, and she pulled it out to get a closer look for the first time since she had taken it.

The purse itself was not extraordinary. It was made of black leather that was worn on the edges and around the clasp. Mia quickly opened the clasp and a burst of excitement ran down her spine as she prepared herself to see what was inside. First she spotted a small silver change purse, which she quickly opened to discover a tightly folded twenty dollar bill and a few loose coins. She emptied the money into her hand and dropped it into the bottom of her book bag. Then, she dropped the empty coin bag back into the black purse. Continuing to search through the purse, she found a few lace handkerchiefs, a set of keys, a pill box, a hair brush, and a tube of lipstick.

"Junk," Mia said out loud as she rummaged through every inch of the old woman's bag. Then on one side of the bag she felt a small pocket that held something hard inside. She unzipped the pocket, reached inside and pulled out a small brooch. Mia couldn't believe her eyes. The brooch was designed in the shape of the letter "M" and was covered with diamonds.

"Junk my ass!" Mia squealed, unable to contain her delight. She held the brooch up to the sun and watched with excitement as the diamonds sparkled and danced in the light.

And just my luck too—the brooch is in the shape of an "M" for Mia Maldonado. This is the most beautiful thing I have ever touched! Just then, Mia heard the class bell. She quickly placed the brooch in her book bag. Then she closed the old woman's bag with its remaining contents, and dropped it into a nearby trash can.

Sliding back inside the hallway, Mia headed to her next class, still feeling elated by the treasure she had found. She was so excited that she had forgotten to have her cigarette.

No worries, she thought, smiling to herself. I'll wait and grab a smoke at lunch. Maybe Lily will be here by then and I can show her my beautiful brooch.

Mia slid into her seat at the back of the classroom just as the door was closing. She couldn't wait until this torturous class was over and she was sitting at lunch with Lily, telling her about her morning adventure and about her beautiful diamond brooch.

Mia was thrilled to hear the bell ringing signifying the beginning of her lunch period. She sprang out of her chair and headed down the hall toward the cafeteria. Just before she reached the entrance, she saw Mr. Carlton walking with his head down coming toward her.

There's that bastard. Now I'm going to give him the cussing out he deserves. Mia stood in the doorway, waiting for Mr. Carlton to approach. Just as Mr. Carlton looked up to enter the cafeteria, Dean Drake emerged from her office right across the hall.

"Hello, Dean Drake," Mia said with a sheepish grin.

"Hi Mia," Dean Drake replied with a smile and walked past Mia into the cafeteria.

Cutting her eyes at Mr. Carlton, Mia turned and followed behind Ms. Drake into the noisy eating hall. "I'll get your ass another time," she said to Mr. Carlton under her breath and headed into the lunch area anxious to find Lily.

chapter 17

SEEING MIA ENTER THE CAFETERIA, Mr. Carlton was reminded that he had a meeting in the afternoon with Mia's mother. He had scheduled an appointment to speak with her about Mia's disrespectful language. He dreaded meeting with Ms. Maldonado, as he had already met with her once before and found her personality to be as difficult as Mia's. This time, he had asked Ms. Drake to sit in on the meeting, hoping that she would be able to assist him in keeping Ms. Maldonado calm.

The rest of the morning flew by as Mr. Carlton met with students, attended the weekly staff meeting, and returned phone calls. Before he knew it, it was time for the meeting with Ms. Maldonado. Ms. Drake arrived at his office a few minutes early and they briefly reviewed their game plan regarding the discussion they needed to have with her about her daughter.

Within minutes, Mr. Carlton saw Mia and her mother enter the outer office of the guidance area and motioned for them to come into his office. Ms. Maldonado, a tall, attractive woman of slim build, entered first. He could feel the hostility that trailed in behind her and seeped through her piercing eyes as they glared back and forth between him and Ms. Drake. It was easy to gather from her attitude that Ms. Maldonado had already rendered her verdict regarding the situation and in her mind, Mia was innocent of all allegations.

"Good afternoon, Ms. Maldonado. Thank you for coming," Ms. Drake said in a sincere tone.

"I don't know why I'm here," Ms. Maldonado grunted as she took one of the empty chairs in front of Mr. Carlton's desk. Mia sat down in the chair beside her.

"I had to take time off from my job to come here. I'm tired of arguing with you people about my daughter."

Ms. Drake continued, "Well, as you know, Mia just returned today from a three-day suspension that I gave her. We need to talk to you about her behavior and her disrespectful attitude to our staff members. This has been going on for a while now and we need to see some changes."

"What do you mean changes? My daughter is not disrespectful to anybody! My daughter says that—"

"Ms. Maldonado, look at these files," Ms. Drake interjected as she grabbed a pile of folders from the corner of Mr. Carlton's desk. "We have sent you numerous letters informing you of your daughter's academic and behavioral problems. In six months, she has been suspended four times. She cuts class, sneaks outside to smoke, lets unauthorized individuals into the building, curses at our staff members, and the list goes on and on."

"I don't know why you people insist on making up these lies about my daughter. Mia is a good girl. I admit she can be a little headstrong at times, but my child's not a hoodlum! I'm a single mother and I'm doing the best I can to put a roof over her head and send her to school every day."

With that, Ms. Maldonado stood up to leave. "I'm not coming down here anymore about this nonsense. Don't call my house anymore with tattletales about Mia. You people are the ones with the problem. Mia is a sensitive child and you people are just too hard on her."

Ms. Maldonado motioned for Mia to follow, and they both turned and walked out of Mr. Carlton's office.

"If Mia gets into trouble again, we're going to have to transfer her to another school," Ms. Drake said calmly to Mr. Carlton.

She got up from her chair and started to leave Mr. Carlton's office to address the many other issues that waited patiently on her desk for her.

"We tried," she said, turning to face Mr. Carlton again. Then she walked briskly out of his office.

chapter 18

SEVERAL DAYS HAD PASSED SINCE Dayton's suicide attempt. The night that his dad took him to the hospital for an evaluation, they had spent hours just waiting to be seen by a doctor. Finally, following several lab tests and a mental health assessment, Dayton was diagnosed with seasonal affective disorder (SAD). Dayton was as much surprised by the diagnosis as he was relieved by it. After his doctor explained the symptoms, which included fatigue, feelings of misery, guilt, and despair, avoidance of social contacts, and even thoughts of suicide, Dayton realized that he had experienced all of these symptoms and others as well. The doctor explained to Dayton and his parents that SAD is a mood disorder in which people who enjoy good mental health during most of the year experience depression during the winter months when there is less sunshine.[*]

Dayton's parents were happy that the good news about Dayton's disorder was that it was easily treatable by exposure to light. The doctor had recommended that Dayton spend a half-hour each morning before school sitting by a specially designed lamp called a "light box," which provided an intense illumination of light to help treat people with SAD. Dayton knew that his dad could not afford much in terms of this added expense, but after spending a few hours on the computer, he was able to find an affordable light box for less than fifty dollars. The doctor had also recommended that Dayton spend more time involved in outside activities to get more exposure to natural sunlight. As a result, Dayton had started to spend a half-hour after school each day shooting hoops with a few guys in the neighborhood or taking a jog around the park before going to his job at the grocery store.

When Dayton was diagnosed with SAD, one of the first things Mr. Dennis did was to scrape together the money to pay the electric bill so they could get the lights in the house back on. Given all that they had gone through, he didn't want to take any chances with Dayton being in the dark again.

Dayton had started to feel better almost immediately after beginning the light treatments. His feelings of despair and desperation started to dissipate. His doom and gloom attitude about life slowly began to vanish and was replaced with hopefulness. During his ordeal, he had missed several days of school, but because he was such a good student, he had been able to catch up in his classes in a very short time. He felt better than he had in months. Just knowing what led to his bout with depression went a long way in helping Dayton to see himself differently and to not be so hard on himself. He had even begun to develop a closeness with his father and over the last few weeks, they had spent lots of time together watching sports on TV, playing chess, or just talking.

Dayton's bout with suicide, however, had had a tremendous effect on his mother. She took to hovering over Dayton when he was home and worrying excessively after him anytime he left the house. She had even insisted that her husband forego some other bills to purchase a cell phone for Dayton and called him numerous times throughout the day to make sure he was okay.

Sometimes, late at night, she would go into Dayton's room and sit at the edge of his bed to watch him while he slept. Although Dayton's doctor had explained to her the reason for Dayton's episode of depression, she would never forget that terrible night when a stranger arrived at their home to inform them of their son's intent to kill himself. So, despite what the doctor said, she wouldn't take any chances with protecting her son, even if it was from himself.

chapter 19

LILY'S MIND RACED AS SHE bounced around in the back of the ambulance. Nanna looked so frail and helpless peering back at her over the oxygen mask that covered her nose and mouth. After getting the phone call from Mrs. Munchie, Lily had raced the two blocks to where her grandmother had fallen. Fortunately, Mrs. Munchie had been out walking her dog and was only a short distance behind Nanna when she fell. After seeing how hard Nanna had hit the ground, Mrs. Munchie had immediately called 911. Then she called Lily to let her know what had happened, and stayed with Nanna, trying to keep her calm until the ambulance arrived. Lily reached the scene just as the ambulance pulled up.

"Nanna! Are you okay? Nanna! Nanna!" Lily called to her grandmother several times, but Nanna had continued to fade in and out of consciousness. Lily grew even more alarmed when she heard one of the attendants say that Nanna was having difficulty breathing.

Working quickly, the attendants had gently lifted Nanna onto a portable bed and into the back of the ambulance. While she watched this scene in disbelief, Lily took out her cell phone and called her father, who was headed home from work. He planned to meet them at the hospital.

Was this really happening? Why hadn't Nanna taken a taxi to the senior citizen center as she always did? What had possessed her to think she could walk to the center, especially with the weather being so cold and damp? These questions spun around in Lily's mind over and over, but just questions, no answers.

The shrill sound of the ambulance siren startled Lily as they plowed through the morning traffic. Although she had heard sirens all her life, it was as if she were hearing the sound for the first time. This time was different. This time it was her family with the emergency. This time she was the helpless relative riding in the back of the ambulance with her grandmother, not knowing what the next minute might bring. Looking down at Nanna's face vacillating between twitching in pain and total unconsciousness, she wanted to scream loud enough to drown out the screeching siren. She wanted to scream loud enough to wake God, who surely must have been sleeping when this happened to Nanna.

After what felt like an eternity, but actually had only been minutes, the ambulance pulled up to the emergency entrance at the hospital. The attendants wheeled Nanna inside and she was immediately engulfed in white and pastel uniforms, the sound of clanging instruments and medical lingo as they rolled her into a room off the hallway. Lily was directed to a waiting room where she sat in a state of terror, waiting for her father to arrive.

A few minutes later, her father sprinted into the waiting room, filling it with the rush of anxiety and overwhelming fear he brought with him. He immediately charged at Lily with questions.

"What happened? How is she? Is she going to be okay?" Questions for none of which she had the answers.

Lily was almost grateful when the lady from the reception desk entered the room and asked her father to come to the reception area to fill out some paperwork. After a while, he returned to where Lily was sitting, took her hand in his, and they sat in silence waiting for word from the doctors.

Waiting was not a new concept for Lily. As far back as she could remember she had been waiting—waiting for her mother to come back to her. Every year on her birthday, she would wait for the mail to show up, hoping for a card or letter from her mother, just letting her know that she remembered her. Sometimes, when the phone rang, as she waited for the caller to identify themselves, for those few seconds she waited to hear the sound of her mother's voice on the other end of the receiver. Every Mother's Day some part of her spent the day waiting for the doorbell to ring and to find her mother standing on the front porch. After all, the front porch was the place where they had parted, so Lily saw it as the perfect spot for their reunion to take place. But so far, Lily's waiting had been in vain. There had been no cards or phone calls or visits from her mother. Still, she knew a part of her would always be waiting.

Settling back in her chair, Lily tightened her grasp on her father's hand and tried to ignore the feeling of helplessness that waiting always brought with it.

chapter 20

A BROKEN HIP. NANNA'S HIP had been shattered in the fall and would have to be replaced. It had been several hours since the surgeon had informed Lily and her father about Nanna's injuries, but his words still hung in the air like a thick puff of smoke and clouded Lily's head. Now they were waiting for Nanna to come out of surgery. Lily and her father had been allowed to see Nanna for just a few minutes before they wheeled her into the surgery room.

The sight of her grandmother had frightened Lily as she leaned over to kiss her forehead before the vampires in head covers and blue uniforms swooped down on her and wheeled her away. Nanna's head had barely peeked out from beneath the white sheet that covered her bed. Lily could see that the vampires had already claimed her as she was wearing an identical head cover and the skin on her face was dull and lifeless.

Three hours later Lily heard the surgeon's voice and looked up to see him standing in front of them. She hadn't even heard him come into the room.

"Well, she's out of surgery. The hip replacement went well. She's a tough lady. She'll have to stay in the hospital for a while, and after that she will need constant care while she's recovering."

"Can we see her?"

"She's still in the recovery room, but you may see her for a few minutes, although she's still pretty woozy."

Before the doctor could finish his sentence, Lily had jumped from her chair and was heading down the hall to find her grandmother. She had heard what the doctor said, but she wanted to see with her own eyes that Nanna was okay. At the end of the hallway, she was met by a nurse who directed her into the recovery area. The nurse led Lily past several other patients to Nanna's bed at the far end of the room.

Looking at Nanna's cobweb of wires and tubes, Lily realized just how critical her condition was. She hardly resembled the strong, self-sufficient woman who had spent the last fourteen years taking care of her. There was no trace of the woman who had spent hours standing beside her over the kitchen counter, teaching her how to make biscuits and homemade pasta. As her eyes darted over the tubes that drained liquid into her grandmother's arm and those that leaked oxygen into her nostrils, Lily feared she might never see that woman again.

"I'm here, Nanna," Lily whispered. "I'll take care of you." Lily couldn't help but suspect that Nanna had felt the same about her when she had opened the front door fourteen years ago and found her in a laundry basket on the porch.

As she reached out and grabbed her grandmother's hand, Lily closed her eyes and hoped that she was having a terrible nightmare. She allowed herself to imagine that when she opened her eyes, she would be back in her cozy bedroom and Nanna would be calling her from downstairs to wake her up for school.

chapter 21

Miki

THE TREBLE CLEF NIGHTCLUB WAS crowded far beyond its capacity. Miki sat at the piano on the small stage and scanned the crowd, praying not to see any familiar faces peering back at her. This was her debut appearance in the jazz quartet she had recently joined. The other members of the group were all men and had been playing together professionally for several years. Miki couldn't believe she had even auditioned for the group, let alone had gotten the job. Best of all, the other members of the group all had other jobs just as she did and performed only on the weekends. Their pianist, who had been with them from the group's inception, had recently taken time off to complete a six-month assignment in the European headquarters of the company where he worked. While browsing the newspaper one day, Miki had come across the ad seeking a temporary replacement for him.

One of the things that had appealed to Miki the most about joining the quartet was that most of the gigs they booked were in New Jersey. This was great for her because the few friends she had rarely if ever ventured across the bridge to New Jersey for anything. This improved her chances of being able to keep her secret. She hadn't told anyone about her musical moonlighting, not even her best friend, Lois. That way, if it turned out that she wasn't good enough and it didn't work out, she wouldn't have the embarrassment of having to explain to anybody.

Miki had rehearsed with the quartet Friday, Saturday, and Sunday nights for the last three weeks and felt very comfortable with them. They were fantastic musicians and genuinely nice guys, each with wives and children. Sitting at the piano to begin the first set of her first professional gig, she was overwhelmed with a rush of excitement. She couldn't believe how comfortable she felt sitting on stage in front of all the strange faces gawking back at her.

Suddenly, the lights dimmed even more than they already were and the saxophonist began playing the introduction to their first song of the evening. Right on cue, Miki watched her fingers strike the F7 chord and everything after that was a blur. She drifted into another world—the world of music. She couldn't remember which songs they performed, how many sets, or for how long they had lasted. All she remembered was the long applause each time they finished a song and how wonderful and energized she felt when the night was over and she was driving back across the George Washington Bridge toward Manhattan.

The New York skyline was breathtaking and romantic. The golden glow of the city lights contrasted perfectly against the blackness of the night. With the mellow sound of Miles Davis' "Kind Of Blue" floating softly from her car radio, Miki couldn't help but remember "Him." Yes, there had been a "Him" in her life.

They were both in their twenties when they met at a summer concert in Central Park.

Miki had spotted him immediately as she sat in the front row of the audience and he played his trumpet from a back corner of the stage. Other than played by Miles himself, she had never heard the song "Blue In Green" (her favorite song from the "Kind Of Blue" repertoire) played so eloquently. He was beautiful. His face looked more like it had been meticulously sculptured by a brilliant artist rather than of human flesh and bone. He noticed her as well and after the concert, he had stepped down from the stage and introduced himself. From the moment he removed his shade glasses and flashed his enormous brown eyes at her, Miki was shamelessly hooked. She spent the next fifteen years loving and hating him, in joy and in sorrow, in hope and in despair.

The first two years that Miki was with "Him" had been some of the happiest years of her life. They were inseparable, spending every waking moment together except for the time they each spent at their respective jobs. On the weekends and sometimes even during the weekdays she would attend his gigs, as she was absolutely his biggest fan. She was drawn to his music like a moth to a flame. In her naiveté, she believed that the sensitivity and emotion with which he played his music was a testament to who he was, to the kind of man he was inside. After all, how could anyone play notes as beautifully as he did and not have a beautiful soul?

To his credit, during those early years of their relationship, he had tried to be the man she wanted: attentive, loving, uplifting, and monogamous. But slowly, the facade had started to peel away and he stopped pretending to be her "Mr. Right." Even then, she still refused to see "Him" for his true self. Her best friend, Lois, could see and tried to share her insights with Miki, but she had kept her blinders on. Like a race horse running toward the finish line, she ignored what she knew was going on around her in the hope that she would win "Him" over in the end.

Then one Saturday evening while returning from a colleague's baby shower in White Plains, her car broke down on the highway. She called her roadside car service, but they told her that they were backed up and it would be at least an hour before they could get to her. That being the case, she decided to call "Him." After explaining her predicament, she asked "Him" if he could come pick her up. Miki remembered his response as if it happened just yesterday.

"Baby, I'm sleeping. I've got a gig in a few hours and I really need to get some sleep. Just call a taxi service. They'll come get you."

Just as she had hung up the phone, a car pulled up behind her immobilized vehicle. The man who got out was well-dressed and pleasant looking.

After offering his assistance, he fiddled under the hood of her car for a little while, and then told her that he thought she had a problem with her carburetor. He went on to inform her that just a week or so earlier, his wife had had a similar problem with her car. He mentioned that he had gone to where she was stranded on the highway to rescue her.

"I hate to see women stranded on the road. It's so dangerous these days," he had said to her.

The real shocker for Miki came when this stranger on the road sat behind her in his car (while she sat in hers) and waited with her until the tow truck arrived. It was at that point that Miki's blinders had dropped off and for the first time, she saw her relationship with "Him" for what it really was—unilateral. Here, some other woman's man had stopped to take care of her when she supposedly had a man of her own. Finally, her eyes were open and she didn't like the clingy, needy, dare she say desperate woman that she had allowed herself to become. Through the kindness of a stranger on the side of the road, she realized that she loved herself more than he ever would, and walked away from the toxic relationship that was slowly but surely killing her.

She had promised herself never again to speak his name. The mere mention of it automatically drummed up feelings of self-degradation inside her that she could not suppress. It would take months to rid her tongue of the disgusting taste that even whispering his name would surely leave there. Her friends were forbidden to speak his name as well since, as did the bell for Pavlov's dogs, the hearing of it triggered a similar uncontrollable response. So this man with whom she had shared fifteen years of her life, the man who she thought she might one day call "Husband" had been renamed "Him."

It had been difficult for Miki to even respond to questions from her friends about the end of their relationship. Why did you break up with "Him"? When's the last time you heard from "Him"? Do you think you'll ever get back with "Him"? To make it easier on herself (and because it was therapeutic for her as well) Miki wrote a poem about the relationship, which she put in a frame and hung prominently on her bedroom wall. In response to her friends' questions about what happened, she had led them into her bedroom, pointed to the poem, and left them to read the tragic story for themselves.

Predator – By Miki Shaw

He had captured her without chase as she stood like a helpless fawn, mesmerized by the brilliance of his beauty.

She fell, trapped beneath his powerful touch, paralyzed by his clever whispers of forever love and undying devotion.

When she was completely full of love for him, his insatiable addiction to self-indulgence caused him to pounce upon her heart and quickly devour every morsel, his vanity preventing him from relinquishing even that small piece of himself which had so perfectly filled her up.

But, almost as quickly as he had devoured it, she would replenish her love for him and place it before him as pure and vibrant as before.

Seeing her heart's relentless ability to withstand this endless ritual, he realized a new tactic was required and decided to drown out her love by immersing it in the scent of other women's perfume.

This maneuver had proven much more deadly, each indiscretion eating away a small piece of her heart until finally all her love for him had been picked clean and laid between them like dry bones, hard and brittle.

As she turned and walked away, the sound of his racing heart echoed in the emptiness which hovered in the space where she had stood.

He knew the spell was broken, and she was finally free.

After their breakup, Miki withdrew from the world, spending most of her time at work where she buried herself in numbers, or in her apartment playing her piano or listening to music (mostly anything in minor). Lois had suggested that she see a therapist, but Miki vehemently rejected the idea, assuring her dear friend that she was not losing her mind. After all, she knew what madness looked like. Her mother had gone mad after her little brother died. No, Miki was not mad (at least not in that sense of the word).

Driving her car back into the city that night was the first time since she left "Him" that Miki had been able to listen to Miles Davis' music without having a sick feeling overtake her. "Well, how about that!" she said out loud with a smile on her face. Time does heal wounds. God does answer prayer after all. As she made her way through the night-owl traffic of Manhattan, Miki felt more peaceful and content with her life than she had in a long time.

chapter 22

LILY HAD MISSED THE LAST few days of school. The day after her grandmother's hip surgery, she became hysterical when her father suggested that she get ready for school. She cried and pleaded with him, unable to bear the thought of leaving Nanna alone with strangers in pastel uniforms who would view her pain as merely a matter of fact. Finally, her father gave in and let her spend the day with Nanna at the hospital.

This morning, however, was a different story. Her father had insisted that she return to school, pointing out to her that he didn't want her to get too far behind in her classes. A few days ago, this conversation would have made no difference to Lily; she would not have cared at all about missing time at school. Nanna's fall, however, had been a revelation for her on so many levels.

Yesterday when she was sitting in Nanna's room at the hospital, Mrs. Munchie came to visit. Since her pain meds kept Nanna sleeping most of the time, Mrs. Munchie had spent the majority of her visit chatting with Lily. She told Lily that she had seen the whole episode surrounding Nanna's fall. The sidewalk had been damp and slippery, but Mrs. Munchie told Lily that she saw a girl walking up fast behind Nanna, and suggested that maybe Nanna was trying to get away from her and had slipped in the process. Mrs. Munchie said she would never have drawn such a conclusion if not for the fact that after Nanna fell, the girl ran up and scooped up Nanna's handbag from where it had landed on the ground and ran away with it.

Lilly had listened in horror as Mrs. Munchie explained how hard Nanna's body had hit the ground and lay there twisted and helpless. She wasn't able to give a good description of the girl because she had only seen her from behind.

"I knew it was a teenager from the way she was dressed. She was carrying one of those book bags on her back like you kids carry for your school books. And she was wearing some of those tight jeans that you kids wear these days. Honey, in my day, if I had even thought about wearing any of the things you kids wear now, my mother would have shipped me off to reform school," Mrs. Munchie rattled on. "Anyway, I could tell it was a girl by the way she was built. Believe me, honey, from the jiggle in that caboose, that was no boy!"

As Mrs. Munchie continued to chatter on and on, jumping back and forth about the kids of today and the kids of her day, Lily's mind wandered into a zone of its own. She thought back to the numerous times that she and Mia had snatched purses from helpless old ladies on the street. Some of the women had fallen to the ground like Nanna. Others had screamed in shock or just stared in startled disbelief. Until now, they had been just faces of strangers, nothing more. But since Nanna's fall, they had become someone's mother, or grandmother, or favorite aunt. For the first time since she and Mia had started their "egg cracking" ventures, Lily felt ashamed of herself.

After Mrs. Munchie left Nanna's room, Lily had spent the remainder of the day thinking back about the women that she and Mia had hurt over the last few months. What if some of them were seriously injured like Nanna? What if the money we took from their purses was all they had to pay for their next meal, or help pay their rent? What if because of us, there is an elderly woman somewhere living on the street because when we snatched her purse, we snatched her last bit of hope for survival?

Question after question crawled slowly through Lily's mind, each one taking its time to torture her a little more than the one before. Watching her grandmother wince in pain that day as she sat with her in her hospital room, Lily knew that her purse-snatching days were over.

As she sat on a bench in front of the school waiting for the homeroom bell to ring, Lily promised herself that the girl who would enter the doors of Thurman High School today would be a different girl from the one who had left a few days ago. Her thoughts were disrupted by the shrilling sound of the class bell and the commotion of noisy students heading to their classrooms. Lily quietly joined the procession and headed down the hall to her homeroom class.

She had just barely stepped inside the classroom doorway when Mia rushed up to greet her with a flurry of excitement and energy. "I've been looking for you for the last two days! Where have you been?" Before Lily could respond, they were interrupted by Ms. Brown's high-pitched voice yelling for everyone to take their seats.

"We can talk at lunch," Mia said as she turned and headed toward her seat in the back of the room.

Although some of the teachers organized their seating charts in alphabetical order, Ms. Brown's policy was to allow her students to choose where they wanted to sit in her class. This privilege was revoked from a student only if he or she proved unworthy. Typically, Lily would sit beside Mia in the back of the classroom. But today, Lily chose a seat closer to the front of the class. I promised Nanna that I'm going to be a better person, Lily thought to herself. I may as well start by being a better student. Lily flipped open her science book and began to skim the chapters she had read for homework. For the first time, she looked forward to her first-period class.

As soon as the bell rang, indicating it was time for her first class, Lily quickly slapped her book shut, grabbed her book bag, and swooshed out of the classroom and down the hallway. She was glad that homeroom was the only period that she and Mia had together. Lily had decided that if she was going to rehabilitate from her bad ways, she could no longer hang out with Mia; Mia was a terrible influence on her.

The problem was that she didn't know how she was going to tell Mia that she didn't want to be friends anymore. So she figured she would avoid Mia for the rest of the day while she tried to think of how to tell her. During lunch period, instead of meeting Mia outside for a smoke, Lily found a bench on the other side of the school building where she sat and ate the ham sandwich she had made for her lunch. She spent her lunch break reading the homework assignment that her science teacher had given the class. Despite the coldness in the air, the sunshine felt good on Lily's face and she was glad to have time by herself.

When school was over, Lily headed for the hospital to spend some time with Nanna before heading home. She was happy that she had been successful in avoiding Mia all day. She would sleep on it tonight and think about how to tell Mia tomorrow that she couldn't hang out with her anymore.

Lily was glad that Mrs. Munchie had volunteered to stay with her at night while Nanna was in the hospital. She had never spent a night alone in the house. Nanna was always there with her. They would typically spend their evenings watching movies or putting together puzzles, a pastime that Lily had grown to enjoy. As soon as Lily arrived home from the hospital that afternoon, Mrs. Munchie rang the doorbell.

"Hi honey. Have you eaten yet? I made extra lasagna for dinner and thought you might enjoy some."

Lily was glad to get a hot meal. As she gobbled down her first bite, she could tell that the pasta was homemade and was almost as good as Nanna's. She and Mrs. Munchie watched TV while she ate. After that, she went up to her room and finished her homework. It had been a long day, and she was glad when it was time to pull the covers back and crawl into her cozy bed. She closed her eyes and thought about how she was going to tell Mia tomorrow that they wouldn't be BFFs after all.

chapter 23

DAYTON WAS BEYOND WORRIED. HE had filled out his application to Harvard as soon as he received it. Several weeks had passed now and still no word from them. He had even checked in with Mr. Carlton, who told him that most schools were in the process of sending out acceptance letters and that he should hear back from Harvard soon. Mr. Carlton suggested that if he didn't hear anything within the next week or so that he would help Dayton follow up with Harvard to see what was going on. In typical Mr. Carlton fashion, he had ended their conversation by pointing out to Dayton that no news was better than bad news.

Dayton was continuing with his light box treatments and was feeling much more like himself these days. In fact, everything in his life seemed to be working itself out; that is, with the exception of Harvard. With each day that went by without a letter from the university, Dayton grew increasingly concerned that his dream of attending that school would be one that he would not realize. More than anything, he was angry with himself for applying just to Harvard and not to other schools as well. He had worked hard in keeping his grades up and had a perfect 4.0 grade point average. The thought of being rejected by Harvard had just never entered his mind before. Now, it dominated his thoughts night and day. The first thing he did when he came home every day was to ask his mother if any mail had come for him. Each day he would get the same response from her. "No mail."

chapter 24

THE DAY HAD BEEN A busy one for Rosa Dennis. She spent part of
the morning at the doctor's office with her youngest child, Lena, who had
suffered an asthma attack. It was close to noon when Rosa returned back
home with Lena, heated her a bowl of leftover stew from last night's dinner,
and tucked her into bed for a nap. All the while, Rosa was distracted with
looking out the front window for the mailman. He usually came shortly after
noon each day and Rosa was so glad that she had gotten back from the
doctor's sooner rather than later.

The house was quiet since the other kids were at school and her husband
was out looking for another part-time job to make ends meet. Just as she
came downstairs after putting Lena to bed, she heard the mail truck pull up in
front of the house. The mailman had barely pulled away before Rosa ran out
and retrieved the mail and began sorting through it as she walked back up the
sidewalk to the porch. Then, in the middle of the pile of envelopes, she spotted
what she was looking for—a letter from Harvard University addressed to her
son, Dayton. As she stepped into the foyer, Rosa placed the mail on the small
table that sat in the entryway—all except the Harvard letter.

Still holding the letter, Rosa ran upstairs and into the bedroom she shared
with her husband. She sat down heavily on the edge of the bed and stared
sadly at the letter. It seemed that the longer she stared at it, the more terrified

she became. This was the letter that was going to take her son away from her and from his family. How could she look after him if he went to school so far away? New York had some good schools. Why couldn't Dayton go to one of them? Besides, now that he had been diagnosed with SAD, she needed him home so that she could make sure that he took his light box treatments and got enough time outside in the sunshine.

At that moment, Rosa felt herself in battle, and the letter that she held in her hands was her sole adversary. Although only paper and ink, it had the power to break up her family. It would lead her son away from his home and the safety that she could provide him and had provided him his entire life. She wouldn't—no, couldn't—allow that to happen. Rosa quickly stood up and walked to the side of the bed where she slept. Using both hands she pulled up a corner of the mattress, revealing another letter from Harvard addressed to her son that she had taken from the mailbox three weeks ago. Then, resting the mattress on her knee, she quickly slid Dayton's letter under the mattress beside the one that was already there and let the mattress drop back into place.

As she left her bedroom and headed down the hall to check on Lena, Rosa felt a sense of peace. She had done what she had to do to keep her family together. The threat that would tear her eldest son away from her was again dead and buried.

chapter 25

LILY SAT ON A BENCH in back of Thurman High school waiting for the first bell to ring. Although the morning was frosty, she was oblivious to the chill. This was the day she would sever her ties with Mia. She had spent most of the night trying to get up the courage to face Mia with her decision. Now it was time to do the deed. Hearing the shrill of the class bell, Lily slowly entered the building and proceeded down the corridor toward her homeroom class where she knew Mia would be waiting. About halfway down the corridor, she spotted Mia coming toward her.

"Lily! Girl, where have you been? I have been trying to catch up with you since I saw you in homeroom yesterday," Mia almost squealed as she approached Lily with excitement.

"Well, I've had some stuff going on with my family."

Before Lily could say another word, Mia had linked her arm inside hers and was leading her down the corridor to their classroom. "Let's meet for a smoke after class," Mia continued. "I've got to tell you about the great egg I cracked the other day." Just then Ms. Brown entered the room, yelling at the top of her voice for everyone to take their seats. Lily again chose a seat near the front of the class. This time, instead of going to her usual seat in the back of the room, Mia sat down at a desk beside Lily near the front.

As she reached down to grab a pencil from the front pocket of her book bag, Lily suddenly sat mesmerized. Were her eyes playing tricks on her? She couldn't believe what she was seeing. Pinned to the outside of Mia's book bag was a diamond brooch in the shape of an "M." Lily stared in disbelief. Nanna's pin! Oh my God! It was Mia! She was the one who had made Nanna fall!

At that moment Lily could feel rage emanating from her toes, seeping up through her body, and taking total control over her. Without any warning at all, her hand flew up from its resting place on her desk and slapped Mia hard across the face, making such a loud pop that it rang through the room like a gun going off. Some of the students fell to the floor for cover.

"What the hell is wrong with you?" Mia shrieked as she sprung from her chair and grabbed Lily by the hair. The room filled with whoops and yells as the girls wrestled each other to the floor, scratching, kicking, pulling, biting, and knocking over desks and anything else that stood between them.

"Fight! Fight! Fight!" some of the boys began chanting. Other students scurried out of the way to avoid being hit by flying books, toppling desks and thrashing limbs.

Above all the noise Ms. Brown's shrill voice could be heard yelling for the girls to stop. It wasn't until a few minutes later when Lily felt the burly arms of a security guard pulling her away from Mia that the blood started to return to her brain and she began to regain control over her flailing arms and legs.

Mia, whose arms were being pinned down by another security guard, began shouting at Lily. "Crazy bitch! I'll rip your face off! What's your problem?"

"You're the crazy one!" Lily shouted back. Then pointing to the brooch on Mia's bag, she continued shouting, "You made my grandmother fall and stole her brooch! Because of you, she's in the hospital with a broken hip!"

"I don't know what you're talking about!" Mia snarled back. "I never even met your grandmother!"

"Calm down, ladies," one of the guards interjected. "Let's go. Dean Drake will have to handle this."

Mia and Lily sat across the room from each other in Dean Drake's office. The security guard with the burly arms stayed in the office with them as they waited for the dean to arrive. She was in a meeting in another part of the building, but had gotten a call about the fight and was on her way back. She had asked that one of the security guards remain with the girls until she got there.

The girls spent the first few minutes staring angrily at each other until Mia broke the silence. "So what if that old lady I cracked on the other day turned out to be your grandmother? Her money spends just like anybody else's," she finished with a smirk.

Possessed again with rage, Lily's body leaped from her chair and flung itself toward Mia. Instead of reaching its target, however, the security guard intervened, placing his massive body between them. He restrained Lily's whirlwind of arms and once she calmed down, guided her back to her seat. "That's enough, girls! I suggest you calm down. You're already in enough trouble. No need to make it worse."

Glaring across the room at Mia, Lily couldn't believe how she had ever been friends with someone so evil.

"What are you looking at, bitch?" Mia growled.

"Not much!" Lily retorted.

Mia rolled her eyes in response, then closed them and leaned back in her chair. Lily turned toward the doorway, expecting to see Dean Drake approaching at any second. Along with the silence that finally filled the room, there was a mixture of anxiety, contempt and, from one of the girls, a feeling of regret. As they waited, each girl mulled over in her head the possible consequences that might be handed out as a result of their behavior. Nevertheless, regardless of whatever else might happen, both girls already knew without a shadow of a doubt that they had spoken the last words they would ever speak to each other.

chapter 26

DAYTON SAT QUIETLY IN MR. Carlton's outer office waiting for him to return. He had just arrived to meet with Mr. Carlton when the counselor was called away to some emergency. A few students passing through the hallway stuck there heads into the office were Dayton was waiting and announced that two girls had gotten into a big fight.

"Sorry for keeping you waiting, Dayton," Mr. Carlton announced as he walked back into his office. I had to assist Dean Drake with an emergency. So how are you doing? Have you heard anything yet?"

"No, I haven't. That's what I came to talk with you about. Is there anyone we can call at Harvard to find out what's going on with my application?"

"Yes, I know one of the admissions officers there. Let me give him a call and see what we can find out." As he spoke, Mr. Carlton flipped through his Rolodex, then picked up his phone and punched in some numbers. "Hello. This is Warren Carlton from Thurman High School in New York. May I please speak with Jay Griffin? Oh, well could you please ask him to give me a call when he returns?" Mr. Carlton recited his number and then hung up the phone.

"I'm sorry, Dayton. He's in a meeting. I left a message for him with his secretary. I'll let you know as soon as I hear back from him."

"Thank you, Mr. Carlton. I appreciate your help. I'm getting really worried since I haven't heard anything. I haven't had a good night's sleep in weeks."

"Well, let's see if we can't get to the bottom of this. Let's wait and see what Mr. Griffin can tell us. Meanwhile, hang in there, Dayton. You're an excellent student and have the grades and SAT scores to prove it. Let's not jump to any conclusions just yet."

"Thank you, Mr. Carlton. I'll be waiting to hear from you. Do you have my class schedule? Can you call me out of class if you hear back from your friend today?"

"I'll walk down to your classroom myself and let you know what I find out."

"Thank you so much, Mr. Carlton." Dayton felt a little better as he left Mr. Carlton's office. His hopefulness gradually dissipated, however, as the afternoon slowly ticked by with no word from Mr. Carlton about Harvard. Worrying about getting into Harvard consumed every molecule of Dayton's brain for the remainder of the afternoon. Finally, he was standing on the front porch of his house without even remembering how he had gotten there, whether he'd walked the fifteen blocks from school or had taken the subway. As he entered the door and stepped into the foyer, he sorted through the small stack of mail on the foyer table. He quickly realized that the stack of mail contained mostly bills and a few advertisements, but nothing for him.

"Mom, I'm home! Did I get any mail today?" Dayton called out to his mother, trying desperately to suppress the sound of panic that cracked in his voice.

"No. No mail for you, son," Mrs. Dennis replied, totally oblivious to how much closer her response was pushing her son to the brink of self-annihilation.

Instead of going into the kitchen to help the younger kids with their homework, Dayton went to his bedroom. His legs felt like blocks of cement as he lifted them over and over again in his ascent up the stairs. When he reached his room, he closed the door and sat on the edge of his bed. He hadn't made it. Harvard didn't want him. Surely he would have heard back from Mr. Carlton by now if it had been good news. His dream of attending Harvard was shattered. How could he face his parents and tell them that he didn't get into college? His younger siblings looked up to him. How could he face them and tell them he had failed?

Dayton felt like his body was moving in slow motion as he got up from the bed and walked over to the dresser that sat in the corner of the room near the window. He pulled open the top drawer, reached in, and pulled out an unopened box of razor blades. Sitting back on his bed with the box of blades in his hands, his brain began to spin uncontrollably. Scenes from his life played rapidly through his head. He saw himself as a three-year old boy sitting in his father's lap, flipping through a book as his father read to him. Then he was seven and sitting at the kitchen table, teaching his mom the new words he had learned at school that day while she prepared dinner. Visions of himself at various stages of his life jumped back and forth through his brain. But in each scene, there was always someone else there with him. He was always with family, never alone. He was always with someone he loved. Suddenly, Dayton felt moisture dripping from his face and realized that his entire shirt was wet from perspiration. Still he sat, unable to move. He literally felt paralyzed by his emotions. He sat frozen for a few more minutes and then he heard someone calling him from downstairs.

"Dayton, phone!"

It was as if the call up to him had shocked his body out of its paralyzed state. His legs suddenly jolted forward, lifting his body off the bed. He quickly stuffed the box of razors into the back of his dresser drawer and stumbled noisily downstairs to the phone.

"Hello, Dayton. I'm sorry to be calling you at home, but I told you I would let you know as soon as I heard anything." The sound of Mr. Carlton's voice was at once the voice of rejoicing and the voice of doom for Dayton. His heart stopped beating as he waited to hear which would be his reality.

"School had already let out when my friend from Harvard called me back. You were accepted, son. You got into Harvard! My friend said that they sent you a couple of letters, but had not heard back from you. He also said that they are offering you a scholarship. Everything was in the letters they sent you. I wonder why you didn't receive them…"

Mr. Carlton rattled on, but all Dayton heard was that he had gotten into Harvard. The legs that had a few moments ago felt like cement began to leap into the air as he jumped and yelped with excitement.

"Thank you, Mr. Carlton! Thank you for calling! Thank you for everything!"

After he hung up, Dayton ran shouting into the kitchen that he was going to Harvard. In his excitement, he grabbed his little sister Lena and whirled her around in the air, starting from the kitchen and ending in the living room. Lena squealed in delight and the other children followed behind them, shouting and dancing with the same level of joy as Dayton.

The acceptance from Harvard had rejuvenated Dayton both emotionally and physically. Suddenly, he was ravenous and took his place at the kitchen table, where he gulped down two heaping plates of beans and rice as he chatted excitedly about his college plans with his family. He knew that he was talking so fast and so much that neither his mother nor his siblings could get a word in edgewise. Later that evening, when his dad came home from driving the cab, Dayton met him at the door with his fantastic news. His father was overjoyed, and he and Dayton talked well into the night while Dayton helped him prepare his newspapers for his early morning route. That night, Dayton slept like he had not slept for a long time: deeply, peacefully, triumphantly.

chapter 27

LILY WAS EXCITED. IT HAD been about three weeks since Nanna's fall and today she was coming home from the hospital. She missed her grandmother terribly, especially the time they spent in the evenings making dinner or watching TV before turning in for bed. Although Mrs. Munchie had been spending the night with Lily while Nanna was in the hospital and her father at work, she was such a chatterbox and would talk constantly through whatever movie or TV show they happened to be watching. Still, Mrs. Munchie was a nice person and Lily appreciated all that she had done for her family.

Nanna's doctor had informed Lily and her dad that Nanna had a long, hard road ahead of her. It would be a long time before she would be back on her feet and able to get around, and even then she would probably have to rely on a cane or a walker. Lily's dad had arranged for a home nurse who would check in on Nanna during the weekdays while she was recuperating. A physical therapist would be coming each week as well to help Nanna get back on her feet.

Mrs. Munchie had volunteered to sit with Nanna during the day while Lily's dad was sleeping from his night-shift job and Lily was in school. They had accepted her gracious offer, and her dad had promised that after the first few weeks of Nanna's return home, he would take several weeks of overdue vacation time to help out. He was grateful that Nanna had a friend like Mrs. Munchie who was there when they needed her. Mrs. Munchie had lost her husband a few years ago. Since then, she and Nanna had become close friends, often spending time visiting at each other's home or with other mutual friends at the neighborhood senior center.

Lily spent the morning preparing the house for Nanna's homecoming. She had actually done a good job of keeping the kitchen sink free of dirty dishes while Nanna was away and had kept her own room clean and dusted. This particular morning, she had swept the hardwood floor in Nanna's room, put fresh sheets on the bed, and wiped away the thin layers of dust that had accumulated on Nanna's dresser and chest of drawers. She wanted everything to be perfect for her grandmother's return home.

Lily had wanted to be there on the day that her grandmother arrived home from the hospital. Unfortunately, her father had insisted that she go to school. She had been suspended for five days following her fight with Mia. During her suspension, she had spent every day at the hospital shooting the breeze with Nanna when she was awake, or doing her homework when she was not. Despite her five days of being away from school, she was still required to do her homework each day. Before she left to start her suspension, Mr. Carlton had to meet with each of her teachers and get Lily's homework for each day of her suspension period.

Lily knew she had changed. She didn't mind doing the homework and in fact had come to enjoy the days she spent sitting at the hospital with Nanna reading a book for her English class or working through algebra problems. This was the first time that she had actually applied herself to her studies, and she was surprised to find out that she was pretty good in math and even enjoyed it. Working through the homework problems reminded her of putting together the puzzles she often did with her grandmother. After solving her homework problems and checking her answers in the back of her textbook, Lily was pleasantly pleased to discover that she missed very few problems. She wasn't a bad student after all. No more ignoring her teachers and her classwork. No more cutting class to smoke cigarettes in the school yard. And most of all, no more cracking eggs on her way to school.

Lily hadn't seen Mia since their vicious fight. She had heard from some of the other students that Mia had been transferred to a school on the other side of the Bronx. Rumor had it that when Mia's mother had arrived at school that day to pick Mia up after the fight, Ms. Maldonado had thrown a fit in Dean Drake's office and accused Dean Drake and other school officials of being out to get her daughter. She had cursed out everybody who came near her and then announced that she was taking Mia out of Thurman High School. Dean Drake was happy to oblige and assisted Ms. Maldonado with the required paperwork to transition Mia to another school.

Lily didn't miss Mia at all. She was glad that Mia was no longer at Thurman and was happy to get back to her classes without Mia there to distract her. When her father had been called to pick Lily up the day of the fight, she had confessed to him how she and Mia had been stealing women's purses some mornings on their way to school and how sorry she was about having taken part in such terrible behavior. Hearing her father say how disappointed he was in her had caused Lily more anguish than any punishment he could have dished out.

Before they left Ms. Drake's office that day (while Mia waited in the security office for her mother to arrive), Ms. Drake returned Nanna's pin to Lily's father.

"Mr. McGlenn, I understand this is what the girls were fighting over. If you're comfortable with getting the pin back, we can leave it at that. Otherwise, I'll have to call the youth officer from the 41st Precinct and get the police involved in this."

Considering what Lily had told him about having participated in purse snatching, Mr. McGlenn decided that being able to return his mother's diamond brooch to her would be leaving well enough alone. Besides, the brooch was Nanna's most cherished possession. His father had given it to her as a birthday present. It was the last gift he'd given her and she would be thrilled to have it back. As they left Ms. Drake's office that day, Mr. McGlenn handed the brooch to Lily.

"I want you to give this back to your grandmother. And I want you to tell her what happened—the whole story."

"I will. I just hope she can forgive me," Lily sheepishly replied. Who would have ever thought that something she did to strangers on the street would have a direct effect on her own family?

"We all have to learn that our mistakes have consequences, Lily. You spill the milk, you sop it up," her father had said. Those words sat with Lily for a long time.

chapter 28

MIA AND HER MOTHER STEPPED off the bus at Castle Hill Avenue and headed down the two blocks to Mia's new high school. Instead of getting up at 6:30 in the morning, now she would have to get up thirty to forty-five minutes earlier to take the subway train and two buses to Pelham High School in the Throgs Neck section of the Bronx.

"Mom, this school is too far. Can I take a taxi here every day instead of having to take the train and buses?"

"Mia, do you think I'm made out of money? I have to take the train to work every day myself. If you want to take a taxi, you'll have to pay for it out of the allowance I give you. I don't have any extra money for that."

I know how I can get some extra money, Mia thought to herself. This was her first day at the new school following the fight she had with Lily at Thurman. Her mother had accompanied her this morning to make sure that the new school had all the appropriate paperwork needed for Mia's enrollment.

Mia noticed that things had changed a bit between her and her mother since the fight with Lily. Her mother never used to say "no" to her and would usually go out of her way to give her anything she wanted. Over the last several days, however, her mother had become impatient with her and even seemed annoyed with the whole process of having to transfer her to a new school.

"Come on, Mia. Walk faster. I have to get you enrolled and then get to work."

"Mommy, I'm walking as fast as I can."

"No, you're not. You're deliberately dragging behind trying to slow me down. It's your fault that you had to change schools, not mine. Now come on, let's get this done and over with."

Mia was right. Her mother was annoyed with her about the whole changing schools thing. Why is she mad at me? I didn't start the fight with Lily. Besides, I gave back the old lady's brooch, so what's the problem? I'm glad I'm not at Thurman anymore. The one person I thought was my friend turned out to be just like everybody else. I don't need her. I don't need anybody. To hell with all of them! Everybody can just kiss my voluptuous ass!

As Mia and her mother entered the front hallway of the school, their nostrils filled with the pungent smell of ammonia. Right away, they both could see it was a place very different from Thurman. They were immediately greeted by one of four security guards, who requested their bags and placed them through a scanning machine that blocked most of the entrance way. After her purse was scanned, one of the guards demanded to see Ms. Maldonado's identification. The guard took a lingering look at the driver's license she handed him, and after returning it to her, pointed them toward the front office with a grunt and nod of his head.

The young woman who sat at the front desk didn't even raise her head to acknowledge their presence. Instead, she continued to sort through the papers on her desk, popping her chewing gum loudly and humming to a song coming from a CD player perched on the corner of her desk.

"Excuse me. I'm Ms. Maldonado and I'm here to enroll my daughter."

"Here, take these papers and fill them out. We'll be with you shortly." All said without raising her eyes to address them.

They had barely taken seats on the tattered old sofa against the far wall of the waiting area when one of the security guards entered escorting a teenage boy.

"But, Mr. Butler, it's just a screwdriver. I was bringing it to use in my shop class."

"TJ, you know the rules here. You can't carry any sharp objects or anything that can be used as a weapon. I've got to take you to the dean's office." The boy was still pleading with the guard as they rounded the corner and disappeared into an open doorway. The boy's voice gradually faded as he and the security guard walked farther away from where Mia and her mother were sitting. Through it all, the woman at the front desk had not interrupted either her gum chewing or her humming for even a second. She had continued to sort through her papers without the least bit of interest in what was going on around her.

After about thirty minutes, the woman emerged from behind the front desk, retrieved the papers from Ms. Maldonado, and directed her and Mia to the guidance office, which was on the second floor at the far end of the hallway. Just as they reached the top of the stairs, the bell rang indicating it was time for a class change. Suddenly, the hallway was overwhelmed with the sound of noisy teenagers, padlocks clanging against locker doors, and books banging against cement floors as they tumbled out of overstuffed locker compartments.

It was as if Mia and her mother were invisible eavesdroppers on the numerous conversations that floated around them as they made their way down the hall to the guidance office.

"Hey Tina, let me borrow your gym shirt. I forgot mine." "Man, I told you I don't have any money—stop sweating me!" "Hey Peanut, you gonna shoot some hoops after school today?" "Ooowee! Sherri, baby, your body is talking to me and it's saying one word—bootylicious!" "Hey man, did you hit that last night?" "Like a hammer on a nail, man!"

Ms. Maldonado couldn't believe some of the comments she heard from these teenage students as they passed by. As she walked the long hallway, she started to feel like a visitor at a prison. A few teachers who stood in front of their classrooms only contributed to the noisy environment by calling out the time remaining for the students to get what they needed from their lockers and get to their next classes. As she entered the guidance office, Ms. Maldonado began to feel light-headed and sick to her stomach. How could her daughter survive, let alone learn, in a place like this?

chapter 29

IT HAD BEEN AN EARLY morning for Lily, as had been the case since Nanna came home from the hospital. Each day before leaving for school, she would make Nanna's breakfast and clean up the kitchen. She wanted to make sure that everything was neat and clean for Mrs. Munchie when she arrived to help out with Nanna later in the morning.

During the past few weeks, Lily and her dad had gotten into a pretty comfortable morning routine of chores. Usually, by the time Lily finished making breakfast, her dad would arrive home from work. He and Lily would help Nanna up from bed and lead her to a comfy leather chair that sat near her bedroom window. After Lily would leave for school, her dad would sit with Nanna and watch the morning news with her while she ate her breakfast. He had bought a small TV for Nanna's room when she came home from the hospital, since it would be a while before she would be able to manage the stairs to get to the television set in the living room. They would chat and watch TV together until the home nurse or Mrs. Munchie arrived to help Nanna bathe and get dressed for the day.

This morning, however, was a little different for Lily. She was on a special mission. Filled with apprehension and yet an overwhelming sense of determination, she entered the main hall of Thurman and headed down the corridor to the security office. As she got closer to the security desk, she could see two male security guards and one female guard standing near the office entranceway, talking and having their morning coffee. Lily stood quietly, waiting for them to finish their conversation. Within a few seconds, the female guard excused herself from the conversation and addressed Lily.

"Good morning, young lady. How can I help you?"

"Well, I'd like to speak with Officer Torres. Have you seen him this morning?"

"No, he hasn't arrived yet. He should be here any minute now. You can sit over there and wait if you like."

"No, I'll just come back later," Lily replied as she turned and started back down the hall toward her homeroom class. She had gotten halfway down the hall when she spotted Officer Torres walking up the hall towards her.

"Good morning, Officer Torres. I was just looking for you. Do you have a minute? I need to speak with you about something."

"Good morning, Lily. Sure, I have a few minutes before the homeroom bell. Let's go to the security office. That way, I can grab a cup of coffee."

Officer Torres was the community officer for Thurman as well as for a few other schools in the area. He rotated his time between Thurman and the other schools, but spent at least a portion of his time each day at Thurman. Although Officer Torres was a police officer with the 41st Precinct, he was assigned as a community officer for some of the schools in the 41st Precinct neighborhood. His job was basically to help the school officials keep the peace in the schools. During the five years that he had been assigned to the school district, Officer Torres had gotten to know all of the school faculty and staff as well as a large number of the students. He knew Lily because of her friendship with Mia, and although they were only freshmen, the pair had gotten into trouble often enough to be familiar faces in the principal's office and the security area.

Lily turned and followed Officer Torres back down the hall into the security office. The female guard and one of the male guards had already disappeared. Officer Torres exchanged greetings with the remaining security guard, who was standing near the office doorway. "I'm gonna make my rounds," he said to Officer Torres. Then he disappeared down the hallway.

Lily and Officer Torres proceeded into the security office, if it could be called that. It was more of a cubbyhole than an office. It was only large enough to hold a small file cabinet that was pushed against the wall on one side of the room and an old, oak desk that took up most of the remaining space.

"How can I help you?" he asked as he pointed for Lily to take a seat in the only chair in the room, which happened to be behind the desk. As Lily walked behind the desk to sit down, Officer Torres leaned against the file cabinet and waited to hear her response.

"Well, my grandmother recently had her purse stolen in the neighborhood. I was just wondering, have you heard of any other women in the neighbor having their purses snatched?" Lily spoke slowly, choosing her words carefully. Her goal was to find out if any of the women whom she and Mia had mugged had reported it to the police. Moreover, what Lily really wanted to know was whether any of the women had been hurt. The thought of causing someone else to go through what her grandmother was going through was more than Lily could stand. She hadn't had a good night's sleep since Nanna's fall.

Although Nanna and her father had forgiven her for her part in the purse snatchings, Lily had not been able to forgive herself, at least not yet. She needed to see if she and Mia had injured anyone. She wasn't sure what she would do if she found out that they had, but she at least had to know.

"I don't remember hearing down at the precinct about any muggings in the neighborhood, but I have to stop in there this afternoon and I'll check for you. Why don't you check with me again tomorrow morning? I'll let you know if I find out anything."

Lily thanked him and assured him that she would stop by again tomorrow.

"Hey, I heard you got into a big fight with your running buddy," Officer Torres remarked just as Lily was turning to leave.

"She's not my running buddy anymore," Lily firmly replied. Then she headed down the hall to her class. Watching her disappear into the crowd of students scampering to the sound of the class bell, Officer Torres couldn't help but wonder what Lily was up to.

chapter 30

"**G**OOD MORNING, MR. WILLIAMS."

Startled, Gary Williams turned from the blackboard to see Dr. Roberts standing in his classroom doorway. He froze, his eyes fixed on Dr. Roberts. The only movement from him was the chalk he had been writing with, which he rolled back and forth between his thumb and forefinger.

Oh God! Here we go again! What does she want this time? Did she find out my secret? Although this wasn't the first time that Dr. Roberts had popped her head into his classroom during her morning walks through the building, his mind immediately went into panic mode.

"Good morning, Dr. Roberts. How are you this morning?"

"I'm fine, Mr. Williams. How about you? How are things going with your classes?"

Why is she asking me about my classes? She knows something! This is it! The cat has been let out of the bag!

"Everything's fine, Dr. Roberts. I was just putting some math problems on the board in preparation for my first-period class."

"Well, I'll let you get back to your work," Dr. Roberts responded with a smile. "I just wanted to check in with you to see if everything was okay. Enjoy your day." Then she proceeded down the hall.

She wanted to check in with me! What did she mean by that? She knows something and she's just toying with me! She knows!

Mr. Williams sat down at his desk and placed his head in his hands. Beads of sweat had already started to form on his forehead, which he dabbed at with the cuffs of his shirt. He could feel his heart pounding like a base drum inside his chest as his body trembled nervously beyond his control. Once he caught his breath, he reached inside his bottom desk drawer and pulled out a hard plastic water container, whose dark-blue color concealed its contents— scotch. After taking two stinging gulps from the bottle, he placed it back into its hiding place in the drawer. *I've got to calm down. I've got to get control of myself before these rambunctious, whiny brats get here.*

Taking several long, deep breaths as he tried to settle himself down, he wondered why he had ever gone into teaching. He despised kids. This was despite the fact that he had two preschool-age daughters of his own. But they were his wife's idea, not his.

Mr. Williams had only been at Thurman for about six months. He had transferred there from another high school in Manhattan, where he had taught for five years. *I had to leave there! They were on to me! They were getting ready to find me out!*

Although Thurman was just as large as his old school, it was much better organized, and Dr. Roberts was much more "hands on" than his old principal had been. She made a point of getting to know not only her staff members, but the students as well. This made him very nervous. *One day, they're going to find out my secret, but it looks like today is not the day.* His thoughts were interrupted by the shrill of the first-period bell, as students began to pour into his classroom.

"Ladies and gentlemen, put a lock on your mouth and put your butt in a seat!" He barked his standard command to them as they scurried to their places. Within seconds, the room was quiet enough to hear a pin drop as Mr. Williams walked over to the blackboard, then turned his stern face to the students.

"Okay, let's begin."

chapter 31

MIA HAD BEEN AT PELHAM High for almost three weeks now, and already she had been in a scuffle with another student. On the second day after her transfer to the school, a sophomore girl whose locker was adjacent to Mia's had met her at their lockers during a change of periods and proceeded to pull out books from Mia's locker and throw them onto the floor. Mia knew that because she was new to the school, the girl was trying to intimidate her. At Thurman, Mia would have been the one doing the intimidating and had done so on many occasions.

"You don't know who you're messing with. I'll kick your ass!" Mia had proclaimed to the girl, after which she had hit the girl hard in the stomach, knocking the wind out of her. This little episode had caused both Mia and the girl to spend an afternoon in detention.

The other girls must have gotten the 411 that Mia was not easily pushed around, because after that incident she had no problems from any of them. At the same time, however, Mia was overtly aware that the girls at Pelham were a tougher breed than those at Thurman, and just as she wouldn't allow them to bully her, she refrained from trying to bully them as well.

Now, three weeks into her transfer, Mia was settling back into her old antics of skipping class, not doing her homework, and sneaking outside to smoke cigarettes. The difference was that now she was mostly alone and didn't have

Lily to hang out with. Every once in a while, she would sit at the lunch table in the cafeteria with a group of sophomore girls who were as unruly as she was, but she hadn't made any solid friendships out of the group.

Pelham High was much farther away from where she lived than Thurman had been. This fact was reinforced to her every day after classes ended when she had to make her long trek home. It began with a long two-block walk to Castle Hill Avenue to get her first bus. This bus took her to Tremont Avenue, which was a little over a mile from the school. Then, at Tremont, she would catch a second bus that took her to the Lexington Avenue subway line. There she would board what the kids referred to as "the booty train."

At the same time every day after school, hormonally charged teenagers from Bronx Science, Dewitt Clinton, Taft, and Walton high schools all converged on the Lexington Avenue line to go home from school. Due to the tightness of space and a little ingenuity from most of the boys (and some of the girls), their bodies would be pasted so closely together that they looked like one large creature with numerous heads, eyes, arms, and legs. Hence, the kids had renamed the Lexington subway line at that time of day "the booty train," where bodies were tightly compressed against each other to the pure delight of some and the overwhelming dread of others.

Mia was glad when she arrived at the Lexington Avenue subway station and her train was pulling in. Today, instead of getting off the train at her stop in the Bronx, she would ride downtown to Harlem. This would be her first time riding the train out of the Bronx without being with her mother, who took her to Rudy's Salon in Harlem most Saturdays for their weekly mani and pedi. She was excited about her venture downtown alone. She was even oblivious to the body parts glued against hers as she stood packed in the train car along with the other sardines. It didn't matter to her that there were no empty handrails for her to hang onto; the crowd itself served as a support structure holding her up despite the train's quick breaks and sudden stops as it weaved its way downtown. Also, the body heat kept her warm, since finding a working heating system on the subway in winter was viewed by most New Yorkers as a privilege, not a right.

When they reached 125th Street, Mia quickly exited the train and followed the crowd that was heading up the stairs to the street. Not waiting for her to arrive at street level, the cold air swooped down to greet her as she navigated the steep, crowded stairway. Once she reached the top and stepped out onto the sidewalk, she saw Max standing on the opposite side of the street near the exit waiting for her.

Mia considered Max to be her boyfriend, although they hadn't known each other for very long. During that time, they had yet to actually go on a date (her mother told her she couldn't date until she was sixteen), but kept in touch mostly through text messaging. A few times, Mia had been able to sneak Max into her old school for a few minutes to see her, or had slipped outside in back of the school to meet him.

Mia had first met Max one morning on her way to Thurman. He was getting off a bus just as Mia passed the bus stop and asked her if she had a light for his cigarette. She had been attracted by his rugged and somewhat disheveled appearance. Because he was nineteen and a high school dropout, Mia kept Max a secret from everyone, especially her mother. Max was the boy that Mr. Carlton had seen her with in the hallway that day, although she had tried to lie and say it was not her.

Max lived with his older brother in a Harlem high-rise. After dropping out of high school, he had gotten his GED and was attending a vocational school located near Thurman High. When Mia was at Thurman, it had been easier for them to see each other. Now that she was going to school all the way in Throgs Neck, this was her first time seeing Max since she changed schools.

Mia's mother told her this morning before she left for work that she had an appointment after work and would be home late. So Mia had planned to hang out with Max for a few hours before beating her mother home. Lately, her mother had been getting home around the same time as Mia and had been watching her like a hawk. It had been weeks since her mother had worked any overtime, and Mia was looking forward to enjoying some time after school away from her mother's imprisoning eyes.

As she reached the top of the stairs, Max crossed the street to meet her and they embraced in a long, passionate kiss.

"Hey baby. I'm so glad you texted me. Listen, my brother is still at work, so we can have the apartment to ourselves."

"Sounds good to me," Mia giggled in response.

"Hey, I'm starving. Do you want to grab some food and take it with us to the apartment? There's a great burger place just a few blocks from here."

"Sure. I'm hungry too. A burger sounds good."

Max walked with his arm around Mia's waist as they made their way down 125th Street. The sidewalk was thick with people going in and out of stores and browsing through shop windows. As they turned the corner Mia heard someone call her name and looked up to see her mother standing a few feet in front of her. She had been in such a daze walking with Max that she hadn't realized they were within yards of Rudy's, her mother's hair salon.

"Mia! I thought that was you! What are you doing all the way down here? You know you are supposed to go straight home from school!"

Mia was so stunned to see her mother that she couldn't speak. It was just as well, because she could see from the inflamed look on her mother's face that she was in no mood to hear any of her lies. Ms. Maldonado quickly turned her rage toward Max.

"Who are you? Get your hands off my daughter!" As she spoke, she grabbed Mia's arm and pulled her away from Max's grip. "I don't know what you think you're doing," she continued. "This is a fourteen-year-old child!"

Max's jaw dropped open, and he looked at Mia in disbelief. "You told me you were eighteen," he stammered.

Mia's voice finally returned and she tried to calm her mother down. "Mommy, we didn't do anything!"

"Let's go," Ms. Maldonado said firmly to Mia, and with her hand still locked around Mia's arm, she began pulling her toward the subway station to catch the train home. As she walked, Ms. Maldonado continued to vent her anger about the situation in which she had just found her baby girl.

"What the hell is wrong with you? I can't believe that you would be sneaking around behind my back like this with a grown man!" (Max could easily pass for a man in his late twenties.) Mia started to interject, but her mother quickly shut her down. "Don't you say a word or I swear I'll slap the taste right out of your mouth! I spend every dime I get to provide you with a roof over your head, nice clothes, and whatever else you want and this is how you repay me? You're just a spoiled brat!" As she spoke, Ms. Maldonado could no longer hold back the tears.

She was still sobbing quietly into her handkerchief as they sat on the train bound for home. Suddenly, she reached up to push her hair back from her face, and realized that on top of everything else, she had missed her hair appointment. Slumping beside Mia in the seats they had been lucky enough to get, she buried her head in her handkerchief and wept silently, uncontrollably, unceasingly.

"Lord, what am I going to do with this child?"

chapter 32

LILY LOVED HER VOLUNTEER JOB at the senior center. Three days a week after school, she spent time at the center helping out the regular staff. Usually she spent her time reading to some of the senior citizens who had eyesight difficulty, or playing bingo or checkers with them. She couldn't believe how much she enjoyed the time she spent at the center. It was her way of trying to pay back for her past crimes against seniors.

After her conversation with Officer Torres regarding any criminal reports of women getting their purses stolen in her neighborhood, he had reported back to her that there had been only one report, but that it had happened so fast that the woman hadn't been able to provide descriptions of the suspects. He also informed her that the woman had not been injured in the incident.

Lily was grateful to hear that she and Mia hadn't injured anyone during their escapades. Still, she felt the need to try to redeem herself by finding a way to help elderly people as opposed to hurting them. Volunteering at the neighborhood senior center presented the perfect opportunity. So, three days a week after school, she would stop off at home to check in on Nanna and Mrs. Munchie and then walk the few blocks to the center, where she would work for an hour before coming home to help with dinner and do her homework. She had fallen into a comfortable homework routine and made sure that it was done before she allowed herself to watch TV with Nanna or play a game of checkers with Mrs. Munchie before she went home.

With the end of her freshman year approaching, Lily had managed to pull her grades up from D's and C's to B's and B-pluses, with the exception of her algebra course. Considering the extra credit homework assignments her teacher had given the class and having done well on her pop quizzes and exams (once she started applying herself), she felt she might end up with an A in that class.

Lily was happy with the way she had refocused her energy in a more positive direction. Instead of carrying her bitterness about never having met her mother around on her shoulder and allowing it to control her behavior, she had decided to free herself from the chokehold it had on her. Nanna's fall had been like a huge, flashing neon sign warning her that she was taking her life down a dangerous road, one which would not lead her to the happiness she was looking for. She had come to realize that her behavior held consequences not only for her, but for her loved ones as well, and she wanted those consequences to be good ones. So she had decided to choose a different path for herself.

Over the last several months, Lily had worked harder and shown more responsibility than she ever had in her life. She had to admit that it wasn't always easy. In fact, it had been easier to get money by taking someone else's and much more fun going to the movies rather than doing homework. She often reflected on a poem by Robert Frost that she had learned in English class. Although she couldn't recite the poem in its entirety, the last few lines had stuck with her.

"Two roads diverged in a wood, and I—
I took the one less traveled by,
And that has made all the difference."

Whenever she felt like falling back into her pattern of rebelliousness, she would find encouragement in these words and keep on trying.

One evening, while helping Nanna change into her nightgown for bed, it had hit her like a bolt from the sky; she would become a doctor and specialize in the care and treatment of the elderly. Before the end of the school year, she planned to set up an appointment with Mr. Carlton and get his advice about what courses she should start taking to help her reach her goal. She wondered if Mr. Carlton knew just how much the students adored and respected him; they sensed that he genuinely cared about them and wanted them to do well.

Lily didn't know where this new road she was on would take her, but she already knew with complete certainty that she was heading in a better direction than the way she was going with Mia.

chapter 33

The DENNIS HOUSEHOLD HADN'T BEEN the same since Dayton found out that Harvard had accepted him. Even the walls seemed to buzz with excitement as the family looked forward to attending Dayton's high school graduation ceremony, which was coming up next month. His father was especially proud that Dayton was selected as valedictorian of his class and would be giving a speech at the commencement ceremony. Dayton's grandparents (Mr. Dennis' parents) would be driving up from Maryland to attend the graduation. After the ceremony, they were planning to have a big family dinner in Dayton's honor.

Also, the family's financial situation had greatly improved. Mr. Dennis had landed a job with a commuter bus service, driving a route back and forth between New York and Pennsylvania every day. He was thrilled because the job paid more than he had been making at his old job, and his hours were from 6:00 a.m. to 3:00 p.m. with the weekends off. This allowed him to get home every day in time to help out with the kids' homework, and he had the entire weekend to spend with his family.

Today was Saturday and Rosa had left him in charge of directing the kids in their house cleaning chores while she took Lena to a doctor's appointment for her asthma. After they completed their chores, he had promised to take the family to the bowling alley for the afternoon. This would be the first time they had had a family outing since Mr. Dennis lost his old job driving the bus for the city. They were all working hard to complete their chores so that the fun part of the day could begin. The house was noisy with the clatter of dishes being washed, the roar of the vacuum cleaner, and children talking loudly as they hustled about the house.

Mr. Dennis pitched in as well and put a load of clothes in the washing machine in the basement. While he waited for the wash cycle to finish, he decided to surprise his wife by cleaning their bedroom so that she wouldn't have to worry about cleaning it when she returned home. Because Lena's pediatrician was across town, it usually took her half the day to take Lena to her appointment, and he knew she would be exhausted when she returned home. He thought he would start by changing their bed sheets.

After stripping their bed, he took the sheets to the basement to wait their turn for the washer. Then he returned to the bedroom to finish his cleaning. He started to place a set of clean sheets on the bed when he noticed that the mattress had a big sag right in the center.

"Oh boy! I really need to get a new mattress for this bed," Mr. Dennis said out loud to himself. He remembered that in a few short weeks his parents would be visiting for Dayton's graduation and would be sleeping in this room. His dad suffered from severe back problems, and whenever his parents came to visit, he and Rosa always let them have their bedroom while they slept on the pullout sofa in the living room.

"Dayton! Dayton! I need you to come help me, son!" Mr. Dennis called out.

"Coming!" Dayton's voice raced up the stairs before him. "What's up, Dad?" he asked as he entered his parents' bedroom.

"I need you to help me flip this mattress over. Grab that end and let's push it off the bed and stand it on its side. Then we can flip it over and put it back on the bed."

Dayton followed his dad's instructions, and together they pushed the mattress off the bed and onto the floor. They were both breathing a little heavy once they got it flipped and back on the bed.

"Here, son, while I have you, you may as well help me put these sheets on," Mr. Dennis said, handing a corner of the sheet to Dayton. As he bent over to tuck the sheet under the mattress, Dayton noticed two envelopes on the floor beside the bed.

"Oh Dad, looks like you dropped some mail," Dayton said as he picked up the envelopes. Bringing them closer so he could read who they were addressed to, he suddenly froze in amazement.

"What is it, son? What do you have there?" Dayton, too stunned to speak, handed the letters to Mr. Dennis.

"These are your letters from Harvard!" Mr. Dennis announced in a shocked, high-pitched voice. "They must have been under the mattress and fell out when we moved it!"

"Mom! She hid these letters from me!" Dayton said to his father, still in a state of bewilderment. "I can't believe it! Why would she do such a terrible thing?"

Mr. Dennis could hear the anger in Dayton's voice as he spoke. Dayton sat down in a heap on his parents' bed as feelings of anger, confusion, and disbelief took turns manifesting themselves on his face. Slowly, his father sat down on the bed beside him. After a few minutes of silence, Mr. Dennis let out a sigh and began to speak in a soft, comforting voice.

"Son, you know your mother loves you. She did this because she loves you and wants to protect you. I don't at all agree with what she did, but I do understand it." As he spoke, he stretched his arm around Dayton's shoulders and watched his son's chest rise and fall in short spurts as he tried to fight through the turmoil that was erupting inside him.

Mr. Dennis continued to speak in a soft, calming tone. "I know everything that you went through, son. The waiting, the not knowing. I know it was a truly difficult time for you and for that I am so sorry. But I know that your mother loves you deeply and she did what she did out of love. I want you to at least try to understand that."

Dayton stared down at the floor and remained silent as his chest continued to heave up and down. He remembered the treacherous weeks he had suffered through, waiting to get that Harvard acceptance letter, the key to his future.

He thought about how close he had come to taking his life during those unbearable weeks.

"I know your mother wasn't trying to hurt you; in fact, it was just the opposite. The good thing is that you made it. You're going to Harvard and you got that scholarship—right?" Mr. Dennis pulled Dayton closer to him and embraced him in a long, tight hug.

"Maybe in time, you can forgive your mother," he continued. "Maybe we both can. But right now, you have a right to be angry. And as for your mother, she needs to be confronted about this."

"I don't think I can even look at Mom right now, Dad, let alone talk to her about this," Dayton replied, his voice cracking with emotion.

"It's okay, son. I'll talk to her when she gets in. Tell you what, you go ahead downstairs and help the other kids wrap up their chores and when they're finished, why don't you take them to the bowling alley for the afternoon? I'll stay here and talk to your mom."

Dayton immediately felt a sense of relief. He didn't want to be home when his mother returned, and going bowling would give him a chance to let go of some of the hostility he was feeling toward her before he had to face her again. In his heart, he felt badly that he was feeling this way about his mom, but his brain was telling him it was justified.

Within a short time, the kids had finished their chores and were on their way to the bowling alley. During that time, Mr. Dennis had remained upstairs sitting on the side of the bed just as Dayton had left him. Although he had concealed it from Dayton, he was enraged about the hidden mail situation, so much so that he knew he needed to take every second of the time his wife was away to try and calm himself down.

He found himself mulling over his past as a young boy growing up in Maryland. He came from a long line of blue-collar workers—good, honest, hard-working people who were devoted to their families. His father had worked for over thirty years in a steel plant to provide for his family. Standing over an assembly line for all those years had resulted in the back problem that he was now battling in his retirement years.

Dayton would be a first-generation college graduate. Joseph Dennis had hoped himself to become the first college graduate in his family. In fact, he had attended college for a year and was planning to become an engineer. At the end of his freshman year, however, while home for summer break, he had met Rosa at a party. They had fallen instantly in love and ended up getting married at the end of the summer. Soon after their marriage, Rosa became pregnant with Dayton. Joseph never returned to college. Instead, he got a job with the New York Transit department and he and Rosa moved to New York where they lived to this day.

Mr. Dennis loved his wife and family and, for the most part, the life he had carved out for himself. But, had he known then what he knew now, he surely would have made some different choices. Foremost, he would have gotten his college degree so that he could better provide for his family. Perhaps even now, a small part of him was living his dream of going to college vicari-ously through Dayton. He saw it as his own personal accomplishment as well when Dayton was accepted into Harvard.

Looking back now, he realized that he had rushed too fast to get married. But he had his reasons. Rosa had told him that she was pregnant. Shortly after they were married, he found out from Rosa's Aunt Carmen that Rosa had not been pregnant when they got married and that she had lied to him to keep him from leaving her and going back to school. After confronting her about it, Rosa had begged for his forgiveness, telling him that she loved him so much that she couldn't bear the thought of him leaving and going back to school without her.

By then, however, Rosa was pregnant for real and he knew he couldn't leave her. Still, every once in a while he found himself wondering how his life might have changed had he done some things differently. As a result, he was always preaching the concept of "delayed gratification" to his children and cautioned them not to rush through life, but instead to take the opportu-nity to live their dreams.

Not long after the kids left for the bowling alley, he heard his wife come in downstairs with Lena. He could hear Lena whining to her mother about being hungry as their voices trailed off into the kitchen. Mr. Dennis made no move to go downstairs and join them. Within a short time, he could hear them come up the stairs and then go into the bedroom Lena shared with her sister, which was the first room at the top of the stairway. Mr. Dennis knew that Rosa was putting Lena down for her nap, and continued to sit quietly on the bed, waiting for his wife to enter their bedroom, where she would come to change her clothes. Hearing Rosa close the door to Lena's bedroom and head down the hall toward him, Mr. Dennis fixed his eyes on the doorway and tried to tame his wildly racing heart as he waited the few seconds for his wife to appear.

Stepping into the opening of the doorway, Rosa was immediately startled by the sight of the unmade bed. Then her eyes widened with fear as she looked at her stone-faced husband, who was glaring back at her in silence from where he sat across the room. The anger that filled the room was so thick that it grabbed her by the throat and made it difficult for her to breathe. It seemed like an eternity (although it was only seconds) that they stood frozen in opposition to each other.

Finally, Mr. Dennis walked over to the doorway and, taking his wife by the arm, pulled her inside the bedroom, shutting the door behind them. Then he slowly walked over to the nightstand by the bed and came back with the two letters from Harvard. Holding them up to his wife he began to speak, in a low tone at first, and then his voice began to escalate with each sentence, gaining momentum and becoming louder and deeper.

"How dare you!"

"How dare you!!"

"How dare you do this to our son!!!" With each statement, he slapped the letters down on their bedroom dresser with a loud pop.

Tears started to collect in his wife's eyes, and then slowly began to trickle down her face. "I—I am sorry," she said, stuttering to get the words out. "I was only trying to protect him. He needs to stay here with his family so that I can watch over him. I wanted…" Before she could continue, Mr. Dennis cut her off.

"You wanted! You wanted! It's always about you, isn't it, Rosa? You never think about anybody but yourself! This wasn't about protecting Dayton! This was about you!" Then he grabbed his wife by both arms and pulled her forward so that their faces were only a few inches apart. Rosa could feel the heat of his anger seeping from his body toward her.

Suddenly, he remembered his four-year-old daughter sleeping in the room down the hall and didn't want her to hear them. He tried to calm his voice.

"When are you going to learn to let people make their own choices, Rosa? Our son has to decide his own future. You have no right to try and manipulate and interfere with that." He had started to regain control over his voice as he felt his wife's tears roll down onto his hand. But the tightness of his grip around her arms and the flushness of his face signaled to Rosa that his rage was far from dissipating.

"I let you get away with this kind of thing once before, Rosa, but this time you almost cost us our son's life."

"*Mi Dios! Mi Dios!*" Rosa began to chant as a flood of tears gushed down her face. "*Lo siento mucho! Lo siento mucho!*"

"I don't know if I'll ever be able to forgive you, Rosa. Not this time. And I don't know if Dayton will be able to forgive you either." With that, Mr. Dennis released his grasp from his wife's arms and stepped back from her.

"Please don't tell Dayton! Please! I'm not ready to face him yet," Mrs. Dennis begged her husband.

As he peered at his wife, his stone face still intact, Mr. Dennis' anger was suddenly replaced by a feeling of numbness. He knew that somewhere deep inside, he still loved her, but at that particular moment, he felt nothing. This realization took him by surprise and caused him to gasp as he tried to suppress the tears that had already formed a watery puddle at the base of his eyelids.

"Dayton already knows," he replied. Then he turned and walked out of the bedroom, down the stairs, and out the door.

It was early evening when Dayton and his siblings returned home from the bowling alley. Still laughing and talking about the fun they had had, they all scurried into the kitchen to see what their mother left on the stove for their dinner. Instead of joining them, however, Dayton made his way upstairs. As he got closer to the upstairs landing, he could hear Lena singing and looked in her room to find her sprawled out on the floor with her coloring book, her favorite pastime.

After a moment of hesitation, he took a deep breath and continued down the hallway to his parents' bedroom. There he found his mother sitting on the side of the bed in the same spot where he had left his father earlier that day. Hearing him enter the room, Mrs. Dennis looked up. Dayton could tell immediately that his mother was beside herself with grief. Her eyes were swollen almost shut from crying and what he could see of them was blood-shot and still clouded with tears.

As he got closer to where she sat on the bed, Dayton saw her searching his face for any indication of how he felt about her. Slowly, she reached out and took her son's hand. In an almost whispering voice filled with apprehension and remorse, she spoke to him.

"Mi hijo, lo siento mucho. Lo siento mucho."

Dayton slowly sat down on the bed beside his mother and put his arms around her shoulders. There together, removed from the world, with Lena's soft, innocent voice floating in and out of the quiet that surrounded them, they cried.

Joseph Dennis puffed rapidly on a cigarette while he stood on the platform at the 161st Street subway station waiting for the Number 4 train. This was the first smoke he'd had in weeks as he was not an avid smoker, and did so only occasionally when he needed to calm his nerves. The fight he had just had with Rosa had upset him tremendously and he found himself having to leave the house. He wasn't able to stay in the same room with her for another minute. As he saw the Number 4 approaching, he crushed out his cigarette on the concrete platform and stepped onto the train.

Although the train was crowded with people going to run their Saturday errands, or into Manhattan to shop, to the movies, to have lunch, or for any of a hundred other reasons that had placed them on the train, he was oblivious to the mass of strangers that surrounded him. The image of Dayton staring in shock at the letters they had uncovered under the mattress kept flashing through his mind like a billboard for a horror movie. He would have given anything for the letters to have been lost by the post office, rather than hidden by his wife.

This wasn't the first time that Rosa had manipulated things to get her way. Yes, there was the time she lied about being pregnant so that he would marry her, but there was another time too that involved their move from Maryland to New York. While the train jerked and squeaked through the dark tunnels toward Manhattan, Joseph Dennis reflected back to a time shortly after he and Rosa were married. They were living in Maryland with his parents at the time while he searched for work to support himself and his new bride. Not long after having applied to the New York Transit Authority for a job as a bus driver, he had received a call that he had gotten the job and was told to expect to receive a confirmation letter from them advising him of when to report for work, when and where to take his physical exam, and so forth. His plan was to go ahead to New York alone and find a place for them to live and then send for Rosa later.

He waited for a few weeks, but no letter. Finally, after calling them to follow up, he learned that New York Transit had indeed sent him a letter and that he had only a few days to report to work or he would lose the job. After his parents assured him that they had not received any mail for him, he turned to Rosa. She broke down and confessed that a letter had come for him, which she had hidden away. It was then that Joseph Dennis learned of his wife's heartbreaking story for the first time.

She was the youngest of her migrant farmer parents' three children. She had been a sickly child due to her asthma and numerous other allergies. Early one summer, when she was about four years old, her parents had taken her to her aunt and uncle's home in Maryland (her mother's older sister and her husband), where they told her she would stay through the end of the summer. They had promised to return for her after the summer harvest was over. But they never did.

For a long time after her parents dropped her off with her relatives in Maryland, Rosa would wake up every morning and run downstairs into the kitchen where her aunt would be making breakfast. Every morning she would ask her aunt the same question: "Is the summer over yet?" This went on for almost a whole year after Rosa was left there. Finally, she realized that her parents were not coming back for her. She spent the next year crying herself to sleep every night.

In actuality, her parents had given her to her aunt and uncle, who already had two children of their own. Although they had treated her well, Rosa always felt like an outsider, not a true member of their family. Nevertheless, she lived with them until she became a young woman and got married.

The experience of having been abandoned by her parents left an indelible mark on Rosa. She had a hard time believing anyone when they said they would come back for her. Since then, she had a strong need to have her loved ones close by. After hearing her story, Joseph Dennis had understood why she had lied to him about being pregnant the first time, and why she had hidden his letter. But this time was different. This time, she had almost cost him his son.

Feeling the need to walk off some of his anxiety, he got off the train at Grand Central Station at 42nd Street and walked the seventy or so blocks to Battery Park, where he caught the Staten Island Ferry. He spent what was left of the afternoon and part of the evening riding the ferry back and forth across the Hudson from Manhattan to Staten Island. The gentle rocking of the boat and the swooshing sound of the waves hitting the bottom had a calming effect on him.

It was late when Mr. Dennis returned home that evening. Except for the light that was on in his bedroom, the house was dark and quiet. Flipping on the light in the basement, he grabbed a pair of clean sheets from the dryer and returned to the living room, where he would spend the night on the pullout sofa bed. He was emotionally and physically drained. The walking he had done had been just what he needed to tire himself out. While he sat on the side of the sofa bed and took off his shoes, he thought about how ironic it was that his wife was upstairs in their bedroom, within just yards of him, yet they were so far apart.

Old thoughts of how she had manipulated their getting married and had tried to interfere with his getting a job in New York came rushing back to him. Now this thing with Dayton just seemed to rake over his old wounds. Mr. Dennis was terrified. Although he loved his wife and had understood why she had done the things she did, he now knew that deep inside, a part of him had not forgiven her. And even if he could forgive her for the things she had done to him, he wasn't sure if he would ever be able to forgive her for what she'd done to Dayton.

Lighting up a cigarette, he leaned back against the back of the sofa while he stretched his legs out across the hard mattress. Sitting in the darkness of his living room, he puffed nervously on his cigarette and wondered where his marriage was headed. Only time would tell.

chapter 34

MS. MALDONADO HAD BEEN IN a constant state of depression since the incident in Harlem with Mia. She was overwrought with worry and frustration about her daughter. Since she had transferred Mia to Pelham just weeks ago, she had already become a familiar face in detention. Also, she had gotten calls from the new school about Mia disrespecting her teachers, cutting class, failing to do her homework—all of which she had heard before from the folks at Thurman. She could see the same old pattern of behavior repeating itself. It was at that point that she had realized all the things that the folks at Thurman had told her about her daughter had been true.

The Harlem incident had really opened her eyes as well, and although she was still very angry with Mia, she was more so afraid for her daughter and didn't like where her behavior was taking her. Although she did not tell Mia, after she had gone with her to Pelham High School that first day, she had called back to Thurman and begged them to take Mia back. They sympathized with her situation, but spouted what Ms. Maldonado considered a bunch of school policy mumbo jumbo about not being able to readmit a student once that student was transferred out of the school.

She had also made an appointment for Mia to see her pediatrician. Next week was the earliest they could get her on the schedule. She knew that until then, she wouldn't get a decent night's sleep. She wanted to know if her fourteen-year-old daughter was sexually active. However, as much as she wanted to know, she didn't want to know, because if the answer to the question turned out to be "yes" it would break her heart. Having spent last night tossing and turning, she felt exhausted as she stepped into the shower to get ready for her day at work.

It had been a long week for Mia. Aside from the "Max" episode with her mother, she had spent most of the day at school yesterday sitting in the detention hall. One of the security guards had caught her smoking in the bathroom. She was glad that today was Saturday and she had two whole days where she wouldn't have to look at those clowns at Pelham. She had hated Thurman, but she hated Pelham just as much, if not more.

She could tell that her mother was still very upset with her about the whole "Max" thing. When they got home that day, her mother had spent an hour ranting and raving about it, and then spent the rest of the night crying in her room. Over the few days since then, when her mother came home from work, she would make dinner and afterwards go straight to her room, where she would lay on her bed and stare at the ceiling. Mia could tell her mother was not in a good mood these days and tried to stay out of her way, spending most of her evenings watching TV or listening to music in her room.

On top of all this, she hadn't heard from Max since the incident. Although she had texted him several times, he had not responded. She didn't see what the damn big deal was about. After all, she wasn't a "child" (as her mother had described her to Max). Why didn't he want to see her anymore? And why was her mother freaking out and treating her like a baby?

Hunger pangs had awakened her early this morning and she had gone into the kitchen to find something to snack on. As she came out of the kitchen with a glass of orange juice in one hand and a powdered donut in the other, she heard her mother in the shower and called out to her.

"Mommy, isn't it too early for us to go to our salon appointments?"

"We're not going to the salon today, Mia. I told you earlier this week that I'm filling in for somebody at work today." Then she heard the water stop running in the shower and seconds later the bathroom door opened and her mother emerged wrapped in a towel.

"Besides, you just spent yesterday in detention. I want you to stay here today and do your homework. We'll see how next week goes and then maybe next Saturday we can talk about going to the salon."

Mia couldn't believe what she was hearing. Her mother had never, ever refused her salon day. Still in her pajamas, she sat brooding on the living room sofa as her mother got dressed for work. When she finished dressing, she went into the kitchen and grabbed an apple and a banana from the fruit bowl on the kitchen table and dropped them into her purse.

"There's plenty of food in the refrigerator, Mia. There are cold cuts if you want to make a sandwich for lunch and some leftover spaghetti that you can heat in the microwave. I want you to stay in this apartment while I'm gone. Do you understand me?" her mother asked in a stern, no-nonsense voice.

"Yes, Mommy," Mia timidly replied.

Before leaving, Ms. Maldonado went into Mia's bedroom and brought out her schoolbooks and notebook, which she placed on the coffee table in front of Mia.

"I'll be calling to check in on you. And do your homework!" she said to Mia, pointing at the books on the coffee table. "I'll be checking that too when I get back. Now come lock this door behind me." With that, Ms. Maldonado stepped out the door, pulling it closed behind her.

After getting up to lock the door to the apartment, Mia plopped back in her spot on the sofa. Then she picked up the remote control and surfed the TV channels. This was not going to be the day she had expected. Already it felt more like a weekday than it did Saturday. After a little while of flipping through the TV channels, Mia was bored. She stared blankly at the stack of books her mother had placed in front of her. Noticing her math book on top of the pile, she picked it up and began to flip through it. Suddenly, she remembered Mr. Williams, her old math teacher at Thurman. He was a horrible person and a horrible teacher. She hated him. As she stared at the pages in her math book, the numbers started to swirl around and made her dizzy and sick to her stomach. She quickly slapped the book closed and flung it into the corner across the room.

Then she picked up the remote control again and resumed her fruitless channel surfing exercise. Watching her fingers press the remote keys, she was reminded of her need for a manicure. Some of her nails were chipped and the polish was fading on most of them. Suddenly, she had an idea. She knew how she could get her nails done although she didn't have any money. The fifty dollar a week allowance that her mother gave her she usually blew on cigarettes and junk food at the local bodegas.

Mia hurried to get dressed and headed out of the apartment and onto the street. There were several nail salons in her neighborhood, so she would go to one of them instead of trying to go all the way downtown to Rudy's. Besides, Rudy and her mother were old friends and Mia knew that if she went there alone, her mother would find out all about it. Instead, she would go to one of the local salons and with any luck, would be back in the apartment before her mother had a chance to call home.

Since it was not a weekday and still relatively early in the morning, the sidewalks were sparse with people. Mia crossed the street in front of her apartment building and started walking in the direction of the subway. Then she spotted her—an elderly woman creeping slowly down the sidewalk toward her. Although there wasn't a cloud in the sky, nor was it cold enough, the old woman was wearing a rain coat, which was too big for her and made her body look frailer beneath its tent-like fit. An egg! Mia slowed her pace a bit, stopping briefly as she pretended to tie the laces of her sneakers. Her heart began to race as she and the woman slowly closed the distance between them. Interestingly, she hadn't cracked an egg since she left Thurman. Since she transferred schools, her mother had gotten into the habit of walking with her to the subway station every morning, where she would catch a downtown train to work and Mia would catch an uptown train to the buses that would eventually take her to school.

Finally, Mia and the old woman were face to face, shoulder to shoulder as they passed each other on the sidewalk. After she passed by the woman, Mia took a quick look around to see if anyone else was nearby. Seeing that the coast was clear, she quickly turned around and darted up behind the old woman. Within seconds she had grabbed hold of the strap of the woman's purse, which she was carrying dangling from her hand. Mia tugged, but the woman refused to let go. She was carrying the purse with the strap double wrapped around her hand and was holding on for dear life.

"Let go, old woman! Let go!" Mia shouted at her.

Suddenly, Mia heard a loud popping sound and instantly felt more pain than she had ever felt in her life. Her body fell helplessly to the ground and she lay there trying to understand the reason for the immense pain that had consumed her. She had hit the ground face forward. The side of her face was smashed to the concrete sidewalk. All she could see were the shoes of the people who had started to gather around her. In between the shouts to call 911, she heard one of them say that she had been shot.

How could it be? It wasn't supposed to happen this way. As her pain intensified, Mia could only think of one thing, and with what little strength she had left she began to scream.

"Mommy!"

"Mommy!"

"Mommy!"

At that point, the pain became too much for her to take. With the sound of a siren in the distance, she succumbed to the loss of consciousness.

When she awakened, Mia could tell that she was in a hospital room. The first face she saw was that of her mother, who sat in a chair beside her bed. Noticing that she was awake, Ms. Maldonado laid her hand on top of Mia's forehead and started to gently brush her hair back from her face.

"You've been sleeping for some time," she said to Mia. "You had to have surgery to get the bullet out of your back. How are you feeling?"

Mia was too weak to talk, and blinked her eyes back at her mother in response. It felt good to have her mother's hand on her forehead. It was soothing and comforting. As her mother continued to stroke her hair, Mia drifted back to sleep.

Ms. Maldonado was still in a state of shock. She couldn't believe that it had come to this. Her daughter had been shot on the street by an elderly woman she was trying to mug. Turned out the woman had been robbed on the street four times already in the last month and had started carrying a gun to protect herself. (She was also a bit senile, which had impaired her ability to use good judgment).

Staring at her sleeping daughter, Ms. Maldonado thought about how very young she looked. For the first time in a long time, she looked like the vulnerable fourteen-year-old girl that she was. She wondered how she would find the words to tell her daughter that despite the doctors' efforts, she was paralyzed from the waist down, and would be for the rest of her life.

Since it happened two days ago, Ms. Maldonado had not left Mia's side. She was overwhelmed with guilt for the part that she had played in leading Mia to make the choices that she had made. Mia was the result of a long-term relationship she had had with a married man when she was in her twenties. She had loved him dearly, and when she became pregnant, she thought that he would leave his wife and marry her. Instead, the man had insisted that she have an abortion. She had made the arrangements and gone to the abortion clinic, but had left before they called her name, choosing to keep her child and raise it on her own.

From the day Mia was born, she had spoiled her to the bone. Perhaps she had been overcompensating for having even considered having an abortion and for Mia's lack of a father in her life. (She never saw Mia's father again after she decided to keep her child.) In any case, when she finally realized that she was enabling her daughter's bad behaviors, it was too late. Now, Mia would spend the rest of her life in a wheelchair and there was nothing she could do about it. She couldn't kiss it and make it all better. As she continued to rub Mia's head, she began to cry as she had done for the past two days—for the life that her daughter would have, and for the life she could have had.

chapter 35

WHILE JOSEPH DENNIS WAS OUT wandering the streets after their argument about the hidden letters, Rosa Dennis was weak from anxiety and frustration. She was glad that Lena was still napping in her bedroom and that the other children were still out. She assumed they were all at the bowling alley, since that's what they had planned for the afternoon. She needed time to try and pull herself together before having to step back into her role as mother to five growing children.

While Lena slept, Rosa somehow managed to muster up the energy to go downstairs and make dinner. She knew that the kids would be starving when they returned home. Kids were always starving. The need to feed her family, however, wasn't the only force driving her into the kitchen. Rosa enjoyed cooking. She found it to be very therapeutic and helped calm her nerves. The more work she had to put into the meal, the more she enjoyed it. Today, she would make paella because it involved chopping up a lot of vegetables. Besides, it was one of her family's favorite meals—a delicious mixture of rice, vegetables, and meat with fresh herbs and spices.

First, she pulled her paellera pan out from under the kitchen cabinet. It was a round, flat pan with two handles, used specifically for cooking paella. As she placed the pan on the kitchen table, her mind immediately flashed back to when she was a little girl, about Lena's age, and her mother would cook paella over an outdoor grill in a pan like the one she had just set on her table. Her mother would always let Rosa help her by letting her rinse the vegetables. Then Rosa would hand the vegetables to her mother so that she could chop them up. That was one of the few childhood memories she had of her mother that had stuck with her. Every time she made paella, her brain would recreate that memory and for a few moments, she was that happy little girl again, before the pain of being given away had left its deep scar on her heart.

As she pulled onions, peppers, carrots, and celery from the vegetable tray in her refrigerator, she began to reflect on the day she had had. Although she had told her husband that she was taking Lena to the doctor, the appointment with the doctor had actually been hers. In fact, she had been to several appointments with the doctor over the last week or so, and today was the day she was scheduled to get the results of all the medical tests she had taken. Rather than worry her husband about what might be wrong with her, she decided to wait until she knew if there was something to worry about before letting Joseph know about it.

Since she was always taking Lena to the doctor because of her asthma anyway, it provided a perfect excuse to get out of the house for her appointment without arousing suspicion. Her previous appointments had been during the week, which made it much easier for her to come and go while the kids (except for Lena) were at school and her husband was working. Rosa was petrified yesterday when she had gotten a call from the doctor's nurse letting her know that the doctor wanted to see her to discuss the results of her tests. She figured that if he wanted her to come into the office instead of discussing the results with her over the phone, it must be bad news.

Unfortunately, today had been the earliest she could get in to get her results. Otherwise, she would have had to wait until the end of next week to get an appointment and she knew she would go crazy if she had to wait that long. The diagnosis the doctor had given her was still ringing in her ears as she played the scene over again in her mind.

"Mrs. Dennis, it looks like you have seasonal affective disorder, or SAD, as it is commonly called." Hearing those words, Rosa gasped and buried her face in her hands. Seeing that she was upset, her doctor continued to try to explain the disorder to her.

"Mrs. Dennis, first let me say that this condition is treatable. It is a type of seasonal depression that usually occurs in the winter months, brought on by extended periods of lack of sunlight."

Before he could continue, Rosa interrupted, "Yes, I am familiar with this disease. My oldest son was recently diagnosed with the same thing. How long have I had it? Is it possible that my son got it from me?" Her voice echoed with both concern and guilt as she spoke.

"Well, the studies that have been completed about this disorder suggest that it usually manifests when people are in their teens or their twenties. More than likely, you have had this disorder for a long time and it has gone undiagnosed and untreated. In terms of the connection with your son, we do see that the children of a parent with SAD are more susceptible to having the disorder." The doctor sat on the edge of his desk as he spoke to her. Rosa was glad she had a doctor who was fluent in Spanish; otherwise, she knew she would have had a very difficult time trying to understand everything he was telling her.

"But my son has been battling thoughts of suicide from this disease. I have not had that yet. Will that happen to me too?"

"Well, SAD does not necessarily affect everyone the same way. This type of depressive disorder can manifest differently in people. You have been dealing with some of the other symptoms like fatigue, mood swings, avoidance of intimate contact with your husband, and some other uncontrollable feelings and behaviors that we discussed the last time you were here. Correct?"

"It is true," Rosa replied as she nodded in agreement.

The doctor then continued with his explanation. "So, although you said you have feelings of hopelessness, despair, and guilt, there is no guarantee that these feelings will turn into thoughts of suicide. In fact, once we start you on a treatment plan of light therapy or maybe medication, there is no reason we shouldn't see these symptoms start to diminish and hopefully disappear altogether."

Rosa spent the next hour in the doctor's office, discussing her disorder and her options for treatment. She told him that she would like to discuss it with her husband first before deciding which route to take. The doctor was very patient and understanding, and suggested that she bring her husband with her to her next appointment. Rosa assured him that she would.

When she returned home from her appointment, the house was quiet and appeared to be empty. She made Lena something to eat and afterward, took her upstairs to her room for a nap. She was exhausted and wanted to sneak a quick nap herself before she had to start making dinner for her family. As she entered her bedroom, she was startled by the sight of Joseph sitting on their unmade bed, glaring at her as if she were an alien from the moon.

She had felt her knees start to buckle under her as her husband walked toward her with the Harvard letters. If it hadn't been for the fact that he was holding her up by both her arms, she was sure she would have collapsed to the floor. All she could do was apologize for what she had done in hiding the letters. She wanted to tell Joseph about her diagnosis, but she could tell he was too upset with her to listen. So she decided to wait and tell him when he calmed down. During their almost twenty years of marriage, she had never seen him so upset.

The sound of Lena coming into the kitchen interrupted Rosa's thoughts about all that had transpired earlier that day. "How are you, my little Lena? Did you have a good nap? Do you want to come and help Mommy with dinner?" As Lena nodded yes while rubbing sleep from her eyes, Rosa pulled a chair from under the kitchen table and placed it in front of the sink. After helping Lena wash and dry her hands, she handed her little helper some vegetables and had Lena wash them and place them on a paper towel to dry.

Lena enjoyed helping her mother in the kitchen. As the cold water on her hands started to wake her up, she began to sing and hum as she washed the vegetables a little longer than needed. Rosa sat at the kitchen table, staring silently at the paellera pan. Then she collected her thoughts and went to the sink to get the cleaned vegetables from Lena. The little girl quickly noticed that her mother was crying.

"Mommy, why are you crying? Are you alright, Mommy?"
"Mommy's fine, sweetheart. It's just the onions. It's just the onions."

chapter 36

D R. ROBERTS WAS RUNNING LATE today. A call from the super-intendent's office had delayed her getting started with her morning routine. It was only minutes before classes for the day would begin and she hadn't even done her usual walk through the building. Walking the building each morning had become such a natural part of her day that she knew if she didn't do it, she would spend the rest of the day feeling as if something was missing, like getting dressed in the morning and finding out later that you forgot to wear your watch.

Finally, after hanging up her phone, she stepped out of her office into the hallway and began her morning observation of the premises. Chattering students were starting to fill up the halls as they pounced on their lockers and hovered about, waiting for the class bell.

She could sense a heightened excitement and joviality from the students that hadn't been present at the beginning of the year. She had gotten to know many of them (a chore which she embraced from year to year as both a duty and a personal priority), and stopped along her way down the hall to talk with students or inquire about their plans after graduation. Others she admonished for running in the halls or talking too loudly.

She also poked her head into some of the classrooms to talk briefly with some of the teachers about nothing in particular, but she always wanted her teachers to feel that she was accessible and connected. Continuing with her walkthrough, she turned the corner and entered another long hallway, at the end of which was the gymnasium and the school auditorium. When she reached the gym, she decided to go inside and check the girls' locker room as she often did, to find the occasional couple of girls smoking cigarettes or hiding out instead of going to class.

Pushing open the locker room door, Dr. Roberts saw that the dressing area was empty and clean. She stepped inside and walked toward the back to the bathroom. It was an attractive nuisance for the occasional culprit trying to ditch class. As she got closer to the bathroom stalls, she heard someone crying and could see a pair of feet beneath the opening of one of the stall doors.

"Who's there? Young lady, are you all right?" she called out as she knocked on the stall door. Immediately, the crying softened to whimpering, but the girl in the stall made no move to come out, nor did she respond to Dr. Roberts' questions.

"Honey, open the door. This is Dr. Roberts and I'm here to help you. In order to do that though, you have to talk to me and tell me what's wrong." The whimpering then turned into sniffing and after a few more seconds, the stall door slowly opened and a student, Tanya Neely, stepped out of the stall face to face with Dr. Roberts. A petite girl with braces and a thin build, Tanya looked more like a seventh-grader than a high school freshman. The whites of her eyes were fire red and her blouse was wet from tears. Dr. Roberts could see that she had been crying for quite a while. Tanya was one of the freshmen students that Dr. Roberts had gotten to know over the school year. She ran into Tanya often as her locker was along the same hallway as Dr. Roberts' office. Many times they would strike up a conversation.

"Tanya, what's the matter?"

Tanya dropped her eyes to the floor, but did not say anything. Dr. Roberts put her arms around the girl's shoulders and led her over to a bench against the wall. Sitting down with her, Dr. Roberts patted Tanya's hand, trying to comfort her. After a few minutes of sitting with her, Dr. Roberts tried again to get Tanya to talk to her.

"Honey, what is it? Is someone sick at home?" The girl silently shook her head, still making no effort to tell Dr. Roberts why she was so upset. Tears continued to stream down her face. Dr. Roberts went into one of the stalls and came back with some tissue, which she handed to Tanya. Tanya patted her face with the tissue as Dr. Roberts sat back down beside her and continued trying to console her. They sat that way for a few minutes until Dr. Roberts broke the silence.

"Why don't we go to my office? Would you come and have a cup of tea with me?" The girl nodded, still silent, and stood up to follow Dr. Roberts.

Once inside her office, she helped Tanya sit down in the chair in front of her desk and pulled out a box of tissue, which she placed on her desk in easy access for Tanya. Then she leaned down beside Tanya and again placed her arm around the girl's shoulders. In a soft, soothing voice, she coaxed Tanya to calm down. As Tanya tried to settle herself, Dr. Roberts briefly disappeared into her outer office. She returned carrying a cup of hot tea, which she handed to the distraught girl, and a paper cup containing some packets of sugar and lemon slices, which she placed on her desk within Tanya's reach. Then she pulled out a box of plastic spoons from her desk drawer and handed one to Tanya. As she sat down behind her desk, she continued to talk to the still very upset girl.

"Try to sip your tea, sweetheart. It will help you to calm down." After Tanya took a few sips, Dr. Roberts continued to try to get her to open up. Tanya was trembling so much that she spilled some of her tea on the edge of Dr. Roberts' desk as she sat her cup down. She quickly pulled some tissues from the tissue box and tried to absorb the spill.

"Oh, don't worry about this old furniture," Dr. Roberts told her. "That's the least of my concerns. Right now, all I care about is trying to help you. Can't you tell me what it is that has you so upset?"

Tanya took a few more sips from her tea cup and patted her eyes with her tissue. "I'm okay now, Dr. Roberts. I have to go to my French class. We're having our final today." Despite her effort to put on a strong front,

Dr. Roberts could tell that the girl was in no condition to go to class, and certainly in no condition to take a test.

"Don't worry about your exam, Tanya. Who's your French teacher?"

"Mr. Burke," Tanya replied, as she tried to force back the tears that had started up again and were drizzling down her face.

"I'll call Mr. Burke and let him know that you're with me right now. You'll be able to make up the exam on another day when you're feeling better." Dr. Roberts could see that Tanya was relieved as she reached for her tea cup and took a few more sips. Then she slowly started to speak. Dr. Roberts could see that she was struggling to get the words out.

"I don't want to go to my math class this afternoon." Her voice was trembling and her tears turned into deep sobs, causing her to bury her face in her tissue while she pulled more from the tissue box.

"Why don't you want to go to your math class? Is one of the other girls bullying you?" Dr. Roberts continued to probe with questions.

"No. It's my teacher." Tanya continued to sob heavily as she tried to respond to Dr. Roberts' questions. Dr. Roberts emerged from behind her desk and, leaning over, she patted Tanya's hand to comfort her.

"Who is your math teacher, sweetheart? Why don't you want to go to your math class?"

Tanya's voiced cracked and trembled as she pushed through her weeping to get the words out. She spoke rapidly, trying to say the words as quickly as possible, hoping that maybe if she said them fast enough, she wouldn't hear them herself. "It's Mr. Williams. He—he makes me stay after class and he touches me and makes me touch him. I have him for last period and when everybody else leaves, he makes me stay after. He makes me do dirty things!"

Tanya then buried her head into Dr. Roberts' shoulder and began crying hysterically. Dr. Roberts continued to pat her hand in an effort to comfort her. Although she was stunned by what Tanya was telling her, she tried to maintain her composure. When Tanya had settled down a bit, Dr. Roberts spoke.

"Tanya, I can see how difficult this is for you, but I need to ask you a few more questions. Okay?" The girl nodded in response.

"How long has this been going on?"

"It started at the beginning of the term when I got him for math."

"Did you tell your parents or anybody else that this was happening to you?"

"No ma'am. I was afraid to. He said that if I told anybody, he would tell them that I was lying. He said nobody would believe me over him anyway. He's mean and evil and dirty and I hate him!"

Dr. Roberts could see the anger erupting on Tanya's face. She squatted down beside the girl and spoke to her in a soothing manner.

"Sweetheart, I know this was very hard for you and I appreciate you for sharing this with me. I'm going to take care of it. I don't want you to go to any of your classes today. I'm going to take you into Dean Drake's office, and I want you to stay there with her today, okay?"

Tanya nodded in response and stood up to follow Dr. Roberts out. While Tanya waited in Dean Drake's outer office, Dr. Roberts spoke with Dean Drake in her office and informed her of the situation. She asked Dean Drake to call the State Association of Child Services, which was mandatory protocol under the circumstances, and have them send out a representative to conduct an investigation. Dr. Roberts realized that this was a tentative situation and that she needed to be extremely cautious about how she proceeded. Mr. Williams was entitled to due process and she knew she couldn't interfere with that. She tried to suppress her own feelings of outrage.

After leaving Tanya in Dean Drake's very capable hands, Dr. Roberts returned to her office, where several people with whom she had scheduled appointments were waiting to meet with her. She couldn't help but feel a bit distracted by what had just occurred. Although she and Reuben didn't have any children of their own, at the beginning of every school year she felt like the mother of some 3,000 children and did her best to ensure their education and their safety.

She couldn't shake the sick feeling she had in her stomach about what Tanya had revealed to her. She had always sensed something about Mr. Williams that made her uneasy. She was reminded of how he always seemed nervous and edgy when she came around him. Some of the students had complained about his gruff approach to teaching, but that was not anything unusual, especially for a math teacher, a course which was not usually a favorite subject for students.

Mr. Williams had only been with Thurman a short while, but during that time, she had sat in on his classes three times (following the student complaints about his teaching style). She hadn't noticed anything out of the ordinary about his teaching methods or his interactions with the students. He had a strict manner about him, but that wasn't unusual for a teacher in an urban school where many of the students had been toughened by their surroundings and often brought that toughness into the classroom with them.

During the observations that she made in his classroom, she had not detected anything in his behavior that crossed the line between keeping control over the students and being abusive to them. Of course, she was aware that her mere presence in the room probably had some influence on his behavior.

Unfortunately, she had over one hundred teachers to supervise and it was impossible for her to monitor each of their classes on a daily basis. However, she made a point to pop into their classrooms from time to time, just to check on them. Mr. Williams had been no exception. She had stopped in his classroom on numerous occasions at various times during the day. Many times she would stop during her morning building inspection just to say good morning to him and to see how he was doing.

Every time that she had done so, she could sense that her presence had not been welcome. Mr. Williams was always very polite to her, but her gut (which over the years she had come to rely upon as her greatest asset) always told her that there was something more to him than met the eye.

Now, her reliable gut was telling her that the awful story that the girl had told her was the truth. A part of her desperately wanted to march down the hall to Mr. Williams' classroom and beat him senseless with his own ruler. But she knew she had to repress her feelings and allow due process to take its course. She was happy that protocol required that because of the serious nature of the complaint against him, Mr. Williams would be immediately removed from his classroom (by his union representation from the United Federation of Teachers) and would be required to report to the district office every day until the investigation was completed. He would have no exposure to the students as long as the investigation was pending.

Still, she couldn't help but wonder if there was anything she could have done to prevent these dreadful circumstances from having occurred. Her heart ached for Tanya and for the other young students that this monster may have molested. She took a little solace in the fact that she was such a fanatic about completing her building inspections every morning. Maybe she had been able to spare this child and others from another episode of terror.

chapter 37

DAYTON COULDN'T HELP BUT FEEL a bit sad as he sat outside of Mr. Carlton's office for what he knew would be the last time. It had been a long, hard year for him and for his family. His graduation ceremony was little more than a week away and he was in the process of tying up some loose ends as he prepared for his farewell from Thurman. Mr. Carlton was one of those loose ends.

"Good morning, Dayton," Mr. Carlton said as he stepped into his outer office where Dayton was sitting and motioned for him to come inside. Dayton followed Mr. Carlton into his office and sat in the chair in front of his desk as usual. Just then, the phone rang. As Dayton got up to leave, Mr. Carlton motioned for him to stay, mouthing that the call wouldn't take long.

Despite the numerous times he had been in Mr. Carlton's office, Dayton had never taken the opportunity to notice his surroundings. He knew that you could tell a lot about a person from their office, but all the times before when he had met with Mr. Carlton, he had been focused on himself and had not been able to see past his own issues.

As Mr. Carlton continued with his phone call, Dayton walked around and slowly perused the office. His eyes came to a halt on some diplomas hanging in frames on the wall opposite the window, and he strolled over to take a closer look. There was a Bachelor of Arts degree from City College of New

York. Then there were three master's degrees. Two were from Columbia University; one was for the History of Education and the other for Guidance Counseling. The third one was a master's degree in Business Administration from New York University School of Business. In addition to the sheepskins, there were several other awards that served as little framed monuments of Mr. Carlton's academic achievements.

Dayton was impressed as he thought about Mr. Carlton. Wow! This man is quite accomplished. I'm sure he had many choices when it came to his career, but he's here working with us hardheaded kids. I wonder why he chose to be here.

In a corner beside the window, perched on top of a little bookshelf, was a bronze trophy in the shape of a runner. On the front was engraved, "Warren Carlton, Second Place Winner, 100 Yard Dash." Dayton was surprised. He had no idea that Mr. Carlton had been involved in track and field. He considered himself a runner as well, but for the most part he preferred long distance running as opposed to sprints. His browsing about the office was interrupted by the sound of Mr. Carlton hanging up the phone.

"I'm sorry about the interruption, Dayton. Please, have a seat," Mr. Carlton said with a smile. "Well, graduation is only days away. How are you feeling? Are you ready to give your commencement speech?"

"I'm fine, Mr. Carlton. I've been working on my speech and I'm just about done with it."

"How's your family? Are they getting excited?"

"Everyone's fine. My parents are going through some issues right now, but I think they'll be okay." As they finished up their cordialities, Dayton took a deep breath and leaned back in his chair.

"The reason I came to see you, Mr. Carlton, is that I wanted to thank you for all that you have done for me this year. Figuring out the whole suicide thing and calling the authorities. If it hadn't been for you, I don't think I would be sitting here with you right now. And you were the only person, other than my dad, who ever made me feel like going to Harvard was a possibility. I just want to thank you for being there for me."

"Hey son, I didn't do anything. You did the hard work and you have a great future ahead of you. Congratulations! I am very proud of what you have been able to achieve."

"Thank you, Mr. Carlton," Dayton replied as he stood up to leave. "You have had such a great impact on my life and I will never forget you." Then he reached out and shook Mr. Carlton's hand.

"I'm expecting great things from you, young man," Mr. Carlton said as Dayton was walking out of his office.

"So am I, Mr. Carlton," Dayton replied looking back with a smile.

chapter 38

WEEKS HAD PASSED SINCE THE big blowup he had with his wife, but Joseph Dennis was still sleeping on the living room sofa bed. Rosa had finally told him about a week later, that she had been diagnosed with seasonal affective disorder, and he had even gone with her to her last appointment with the doctor. She had started treatment about two weeks ago and seemed to be feeling better.

Still, he slept on the sofa. He understood the disorder well enough. After Dayton was diagnosed with it, he had spent some time researching SAD and absorbing as much information about it as possible. But there was one question he was still struggling with; what portion of his wife's past behavior had been caused by SAD, and what could be attributed to her own personality? So, until he could come to grips with it all, he slept on the sofa.

It was late afternoon when he arrived home from work. On his way into the house, he stopped to grab the mail out of the mailbox. This was a chore that Rosa had given up. Perhaps she was afraid she might be tempted again to interfere with the mail getting to its intended party. Whatever the case, she had gotten into the habit of leaving the mail in the mailbox for him to pick up, unless one of the children remembered to bring it inside. Either way, she kept her distance from the mail, as if the white envelopes were poisonous snakes ready to strike her with their deadly venom if she got anywhere within reach.

As he opened the front door, he dropped the mail on the foyer table and went into the kitchen to check on the kids. All but Dayton were sitting at the kitchen table playing a game of Scrabble. He quickly learned from them that Dayton was upstairs working on his speech for the graduation ceremony. He could tell that the younger kids were glad that school was out for them for the summer. Otherwise, instead of sitting at the table playing games, they would be completing homework assignments.

Rosa wouldn't be home until later because she had taken Lena to a late afternoon doctor's appointment (for real this time). She had left dinner on the stove for them. Joseph Dennis was exhausted from his long day. He loved his early bird work schedule, but some days when he got home, he needed to take a shower to revive himself. Today was one of those days.

"I'll be back in minute, guys. I want to take a quick shower before dinner," he said as he turned and exited the kitchen. The kids were so engrossed in their game he doubted if they had even heard what he said. As he entered the foyer, he remembered the mail and retrieved it from its resting place on the foyer table. Taking it with him into the living room, he plopped down on the sofa. He hadn't noticed before, but even when the sofa bed was folded into a couch, it was hard and uncomfortable.

He had fibbed to the kids (although Dayton knew the real reason), telling them that he was sleeping on the sofa because the mattress upstairs was worn out and that the one on the sofa bed felt better on his back. The mattress upstairs was indeed worn out, but the rest of his explanation was far from the truth. Sleeping on the sofa bed was like sleeping on a big piece of concrete. It had been okay for a few days here and there whenever they had house guests. But after having slept on it for the last few weeks, he was sure that a bed of nails would be more comfortable.

As he started going through the mail, he immediately noticed a handwritten envelope that was addressed to him. He didn't recognize the handwriting and was immediately curious as to who could be writing to him. In fact, the only personal letters he ever received were the ones he got each year at Christmas time from his cousin Willie who lived in Alaska and was always inviting him to come for a visit. He quickly opened the letter and started to read.

Dear Joseph,

I know it has been a long time since all of us have been in touch. I am writing to you directly because I know that Rosa hasn't wanted to have much to do with me since years ago when I told you she pretended to be pregnant so you would marry her. I am praying that this letter finds you, Rosa, and your family well.

It is with great sadness that I am writing to you now. I want to let Rosa know that my loving sister, her mother Louisa, has passed away. She had been very ill and suffered for many years. I think that death came as a relief to her. She died last week and her body was cremated. This is what she wanted.

There are many things that I must now tell Rosa about how she came to live with me and my family. Louisa died from diabetes, a disease that she had been fighting most of her life. In fact, when Rosa came to live with us in Maryland, her mother was already starting to go blind from the disease and could not take care of a small child. Rosa's brother and sister had stayed with their parents for a little while longer because they were older and could do more for themselves, but eventually as Louisa's health grew worse, they were sent to live with their father's relatives.

Louisa had never planned to send her children away for good. She had wanted some time to adjust to being blind, and then had planned to bring her children back to live together as a family. Unfortunately, after she had grown accustomed to her blindness, her disease became worse and she lost her leg. Not long after that, she lost the other one.

She did not want her children to see her as half a woman. It was very difficult for her, but she wanted them to remember her the way she had been when they were all together. While she was alive, she had sworn me to secrecy and had asked me never to tell Rosa what happened until she had passed away. It was hard for me during all those years not to tell Rosa, but I had made a promise to my sister. It is bad luck to break a promise to someone who is dying.

Before she died, she asked me to tell Rosa that she never stopped loving her and that she was sorry that she could not take care of her. She asked that Rosa find it in her heart to forgive her for the choices that she made. I hope that she can forgive us both.

Joseph, I am sure that Rosa will need a strong shoulder to lean on when she gets this letter and reads of these things.

I will pray that God gives to both of you, strength and the power to forgive.

Lovingly,

Aunt Carmen

After reading the letter, Joseph Dennis folded it and placed it on the coffee table in front of him. Then he pulled out a cigarette and smoked it while he tried to collect the numerous thoughts that flooded his brain. He was oblivious to the world around him. The noise of the city faded out along with the sound of his children playing Scrabble in the kitchen. All he could hear was the sound of his breath as he inhaled and exhaled puff after puff from his cigarette. When he had puffed his way down to the cigarette butt, he lit another one and repeated his motions until he had puffed away that cigarette as well. Then, slowly, he stood up and let out a long sigh. Before he left the living room, he gathered up his pillow and sheets from the sofa, placed them under his arms and headed upstairs to his bedroom with the letter in his hand.

chapter 39

THE HALLWAYS AT THURMAN HIGH were empty and quiet. With the end of the school year only days away, today had been only a half day for the students; they had not lingered in vacating the premises promptly at noon. The faculty spent the afternoon finalizing their paperwork for the end of the year. Now it was late afternoon and faculty members were starting to gather in the school cafeteria for an end-of-the-year party hosted by Dr. Roberts. She hosted a party at the end of every school year to show her appreciation to her staff for their hard work during the year.

Mr. Carlton sat in his office finishing up some last-minute paperwork. Suddenly, he stopped what he was doing, leaned back in his chair, and let out a deep sigh. Slowly, he opened the top drawer of his desk and pulled out a letter addressed to him from District Five of New York City Public Schools. He opened the letter and read the first sentence again for what had to be the hundredth time.

Dear Mr. Carlton:

Congratulations! This letter confirms that you have been selected to fill the opening as principal at PS 200.

Mr. Carlton had been thrilled last week when he received the letter. But since then, things had changed. For one thing, he hadn't been able to shake from his mind the conversations he had earlier in the week with some of the

Thurman students. The conversation he had with Dayton Dennis, for example. Dayton's expression of gratitude and appreciation to him had moved him deeply and had even started to stir in him some of that old passion for his field of work that he hadn't felt in a very long time.

Also, that same day, Lily McGlenn had come to see him after having decided that she wanted to become a doctor. He had spent some time helping her select her courses for next year. He couldn't believe the about-face this young lady had made in her behavior. He remembered when she was cutting class and acting out with Mia Maldonado. He couldn't believe the 360-degree change he saw in her. Now she had a positive attitude about school and was a hard-working student. It was like talking to a different person.

The horrible news about Mia had already made its way back to her former classmates and faculty at Thurman. Mr. Carlton was greatly saddened to hear about what had happened to her. He couldn't help but wish that Mia had chosen a different path for herself. During his meeting with Lily, he had inquired as to whether she had heard the tragic news about her former running buddy.

"Yes, I heard. Like my grandmother said, but for the grace of God, it could have been me," Lily had said. Mr. Carlton could hear a crack in her voice as she responded. Then she and Mr. Carlton had continued their discussion about her courses for next year.

When he had informed Lily that if she wanted to become a doctor, she would have to increase her courses in science and math, she had just smiled and assured him that she was up for the challenge. He was convinced that she was. Before Lily left his office that day, she thanked him for his help and told him that she was looking forward to continuing to get his advice during her remaining years at Thurman. Then she told him something that really stuck with him.

"You really care about us students, Mr. Carlton, and want us to do well," Lily had said to him. Mr. Carlton realized for the first time that the truth of her statement had never changed for him.

Over the last week, with the end of the school year just days away, several other students had stopped by his office with similar expressions of thankfulness to him for his help during the course of the year. Since then, every time he looked at the letter containing the job offer to become a principal, he felt less and less excited about the opportunity. He had gone through a pro and con list over and over in his head, but what it really boiled down to was what he felt in his soul.

The fact that the new job opportunity was at an elementary school surprisingly turned out to be an important factor for him to consider in making his decision. The fact that the school was located much closer to his apartment turned out not to be as important to him as he had thought. Regardless of the number of times he compared the new job to his current job, the pros of his current job seemed to be what stuck out for him the most.

Pro: As a guidance counselor, I get to work with the students on an individual level and have a better opportunity to make a greater impact on them.

Pro: By the time they reach high school, students are more mature and usually have a better idea of what they want to do in their careers. Therefore, I'm able to spend a greater percentage of my time actually providing coaching and career counseling as opposed to handling behavioral problems.

Pro: A guidance counselor spends more time interacting with the students, as opposed to the principal's role which requires more time dealing with members of the school board and handling administrative details.

After reflecting on his recent conversations with his students, Mr. Carlton realized for the first time during his first year at Thurman that his presence had made a difference. This revelation, along with his job comparison list (which seemed to favor him remaining at Thurman), had caused him to do a great deal of tossing and turning over the last several nights. He had thought about the salary limitations of his job as well, but when it really came down to it, he realized that the desire to make a higher income had been his ex-wife, Nona's, issue, not his. Having a swanky apartment over on the East Side had been her dream and he realized now that it had not been a dream that they shared. He preferred to live a simple, uncomplicated life. Over the last several years, he had been able to stash away some money in savings and was living comfortably enough.

He stared again at the job offer letter he held in his hands. Then he did something he never thought he would do in a million years. After refolding the letter and stuffing it back into its envelope, he pulled out his wastepaper basket from beneath his desk and dropped the letter inside. His mind immediately rushed to the scene from *To Sir With Love*, where the main character, a teacher, turned down a big corporate job to stay and teach the kids. He had always thought that guy's decision was crazy and couldn't understand it. Now he was that guy and he understood it very well. He smiled as an overwhelming sense of relief flooded his brain. Looking at his watch, he realized it was time for him to go to the cafeteria for the faculty party.

Most of the faculty members were already in the cafeteria when Mr. Carlton arrived there to join them. On one side of the room was a long table covered with a white tablecloth. Above the table was a large sign that read: "Thanks for a Successful Year!" Laid out on the table were several very large hoagie sandwiches and several large pizzas. Sitting on the floor at the end of the table was a huge ice bin loaded beyond its capacity with canned sodas and bottled water. A line had already started to form at the food table.

Suddenly, Mr. Carlton heard music—beautiful piano music. He quickly traced the room with his eyes until they landed on a woman sitting behind a keyboard on the other side of the room. She seemed to be in her own world as her fingers glided back and forth over the keys. A crowd of people had filled the tables closest to where she was located and quietly listened to her play as they nibbled on their food. No one was talking. They were fixated on the piano lady.

Mr. Carlton took the last empty chair at the tables near the keyboard and watched the woman play. He couldn't take his eyes off her. She played as if she were born to play the piano. On top of that, she was an elegantly beautiful woman and radiated something in her music that was profoundly genuine. After she had played several songs, she got up from the keyboard and walked toward Dr. Roberts, who was standing near the food table chatting with a group of teachers. On her way the woman stopped and reached into the bin to grab a bottle of water. Dr. Roberts motioned for her to join them and then proceeded to introduce her to the group of teachers who were standing with her. Mr. Carlton got up and walked over to where they were. As he got closer to where they were standing, Dr. Roberts looked up and greeted him.

"Good afternoon, Mr. Carlton. I'm glad you made it," she said with a smile.

"Oh, I wouldn't miss it, Dr. Roberts. Everything looks wonderful."

"I'd like you to meet my good friend Miki Shaw," Dr. Roberts continued as she motioned toward the woman standing beside her. "Miki, this is Mr. Carlton, one of our best guidance counselors. He just finished his first year here with us."

"Please call me Warren," said Mr. Carlton, shaking Miki's hand. As they exchanged cordialities, Mr. Carlton couldn't help but notice Miki's beautiful brown eyes and perfect white smile. As their hands met, he felt a strange connection between them. He smiled and envisioned that if they had been characters in a cartoon, a bolt of lightning would have gone through their palms as they touched and a message balloon would be hanging above them which read "Pow Wee!" He continued to smile, as his vision had reminded him that he spent too many Saturday mornings in his apartment watching cartoons.

During the rest of the afternoon, Mr. Carlton made his rounds and spent a little time mingling with some of his colleagues. Every chance he got, however, he found himself drifting over to where Miki was playing the keyboard. He couldn't take his eyes off her. Aside from being a beautiful woman, there was something else about her that was drawing him to her. He hadn't made a connection like that with a woman in quite some time.

He had been divorced for several years now, but hadn't dated much since then. Though his friends had coaxed him into going on a blind date or two over the years, he found that he was out of touch with the way single people seemed to progress so rapidly through courtship these days. He considered himself an old-fashioned guy who believed in getting to know a person before becoming intimate with them. The concept of recreational lovemaking was foreign to him. Moreover, he was an incurable romantic. In fact, his college girlfriend and his ex-wife were the only two women with whom he had ever been intimate. They both had broken his heart. His current state of celibacy was a constant source of ribbing from his male friends. "Man, New York City is filled to the brim with gorgeous women and you're not hitting any?" He would just ignore them. He was a man who fell in love slowly and deeply. When the right woman came along, he knew he would feel it.

After spending most of his time at the end-of-year party watching Miki, when things started to wrap up and most of the faculty had said their good-byes to each other and left, he invited Miki out for a cup of coffee. He was delighted when she accepted. After finding out that she lived in Midtown, he suggested that they go to a restaurant in Midtown so that it would be easier for her to get home afterward.

Miki took him to a nice little bistro just a few blocks from her apartment and after getting comfortable at a quiet little table in the back of the room, they ordered dessert and coffee. They spent the next two hours sipping coffee, each of them trying to make dents in the two largest pieces of coconut cream pie either of them had ever seen. Their conversation was light and easy and they were both very comfortable with each other. Warren listened with interest as Miki shared stories about her childhood growing up in New York. She even told him about her little brother getting shot down in the street after being mistaken as a member of a street gang. When she said the gang members who killed him called themselves the Doberman Pinschers, Warren dropped his fork on his plate and stared at her in disbelief.

When he could summon up his voice, he shared with her the story of his little brother and how he had found him dead in their basement from an overdose of drugs. He told her that when he and his mother had gone through his little brother's things, he had found several handguns in the back of his dresser drawer, along with a belt buckle which had a Doberman carved on the front. On the back was an engraving which read: "Doberman Forever." It wasn't until then that they realized his little brother had been a gang member.

Although the temperature inside the restaurant was quite comfortable, he noticed that Miki was shivering when he finished telling his story. He took off his jacket and wrapped it around her shoulders. When she asked him what year his brother had died, he knew they were thinking the same thing. Their brothers had died the same year, hers only three months before his. His brother had been in the gang that had senselessly cut her brother down in the street. It was even plausible that his brother was the one who pulled the trigger, or was there when it happened. He knew the same thoughts were running through Miki's mind.

Miki was quiet as she continued to look down at her coffee. Then she took a few more sips from her cup and slowly set her cup back down on the table. She seemed to be in deep thought. After a few more minutes of silence she reached across the table and rubbed Warren's hand.

"Both of our brothers were victims of gang violence," she said in a soft voice. "It just caught up with them in different ways." Warren was at a loss for words. He didn't know how to respond. But at that moment, he knew she was a special person and he felt a connection with her like he had never felt with anyone in his life.

It had started to get dark when they stepped out of the restaurant. Warren walked with Miki to her apartment building and gave her a hug as they said goodnight in the lobby. Before he left her, he asked if he could call her sometime and she had smiled and given him her number.

As he walked down the street to catch the subway home, Warren reflected on the long day he had had. He had discovered that his job wasn't meaningless after all and that he had made a difference in the lives of others. He had also met the woman who just might possibly be his "Ms. Right." Stepping down onto the subway platform to wait for his train, he felt better than he had felt in a long time. It had been a good day.

After Warren dropped Miki off at her apartment, she reflected back over her day and the time they had spent together. She was surprised that she had told him so much about herself so soon. She was a very private person and it typically took her a while before she could open up to anyone. She had even told him about Alexy. Other than with Lois, her brother's death was something she never spoke about with anyone. But she could sense that there was something different about this man. Even though they had just met, she felt as if she had known him for a lot longer.

As she kicked off her shoes and settled back on her sofa, she began flipping through pages of music that she had been practicing for a gig that the quartet had coming up on the weekend. A week earlier, at their monthly dinner on Thursday evening, she told Lois about her moonlighting with the quartet. Her best friend had been excited and thrilled that she was finally sharing her musical gift with someone besides her. Miki felt better than she had felt in a long time. She was glad she had volunteered to play for Lois' end-of-year party. It was no Rockefeller Center, but it felt wonderful to have brought her musical talent out of the closet.

chapter 40

ALTHOUGH IT WAS SATURDAY, LOIS Roberts got up at her usual time and prepared herself to go in to her office at Thurman High. Reuben woke up just long enough to give her a kiss goodbye and she promised she'd be back by noon so that they could go to brunch, a Saturday ritual that they had enjoyed since they got married years ago.

Just a few days remained and the school year would be over. She was looking forward to having some time in the summer to take in a few Broadway shows, catch up on her reading, and go on vacation with Reuben—not necessarily in that order. As she walked through the school's empty hallways to her office, Dr. Roberts felt a bit fatigued. If these walls could talk, she thought, they would tell me what a year it's been. The graduation ceremony for the senior class had been held yesterday evening and had gone very nicely. The class of over three hundred students had walked across the stage one by one and she had handed each of them their diploma, shook their hand, and wished them well. It was an enjoyable chore, yet tremendously time consuming.

After plopping down at her desk, she could feel what little energy she had left slowly seeping away from her and got up to make herself a cup of tea. Returning to her chair, she started to flip through the stack of papers that her assistant had placed in a neat pile on the top of her desk. After sifting through final report cards, lesson plans, and a few scattered letters here and there from parents either condemning or praising her for her work, she leaned back in her chair and closed her eyes.

It had been a long and exhausting year. As she reflected back, she remembered both the sorrows and the triumphs. She thought about yesterday's graduation ceremony and the wonderful speech that Dayton Dennis had given. Something he said had stuck with her and she pondered over it even now. He said: "Having a dream is an opportunity; living a dream is a choice." Listening to him yesterday as he spoke before an auditorium filled to capacity, she couldn't believe that this was the same young man who only months ago had left a suicide note under Mr. Carlton's door. Now he was on his way to attaining his dream of attending Harvard and she suspected that his future would hold great things. Watching him walk off the stage to the sound of a thunderous standing ovation, she was proud of him and was glad that he had chosen to live his dream.

A week or so before the party she gave for her staff, Mr. Carlton met with her to inform her of the job offer he had received to become a principal at an elementary school in Manhattan. Mr. Carlton was one of the individuals on her staff whom she admired most. Not only was he very skilled at his job and a true professional, he was also a person who cared about his students and encouraged them not to be limited by their urban surroundings. In fact, before he came to Thurman, it had not been a school that was on the radar of the Ivy League schools. He had worked hard in a very short time to build relationships with these schools so that Thurman students could have broader options in choices for colleges.

When Mr. Carlton discussed the job opportunity with her, he told her how he had been wrestling with himself about whether or not to take it. Dr. Roberts told him that she would support him in whatever he decided and suggested that he take his time and make the decision that was the best for him. Although she tried not to sway him in either direction, she was thrilled when he met with her yesterday to tell her of his decision to stay at Thurman. She was also delighted to learn (though he hadn't mentioned it during their meeting yesterday), that he had clicked with her best friend, Miki. She heard from Miki that over the weekend, he would be attending a gig the quartet was working in New Brunswick, New Jersey. Miki had sounded like a giddy schoolgirl when she shared with Lois how he had no problem driving all the way to New Jersey to see her perform, just because she had invited him. She smiled when she thought about how happy Miki sounded. She hadn't heard her sound so happy in a very long time.

Opening her eyes, Dr. Roberts sat up in her chair and continued to sort through her papers. After a while, she got up and went into her outer office for another cup of tea. On her way back to her desk, she noticed a piece of paper sitting in her fax machine. She pulled the paper out of the machine and saw that it was from the Special Investigations Section of the Board of Education. Right away, she knew it was about the molestation complaint involving Mr. Williams.

After they called the authorities to follow up on what Tanya had shared with her that day in her office, an investigator had come to the school that same day. Dr. Roberts was glad that the response had been a swift one. The investigator spent quite some time talking with Tanya alone, and apparently her experience in this type of matter had led her to believe that there was sufficient cause to get the police involved. The police arrested Mr. Williams at his home that evening while he was having dinner with his wife and two little girls. What was really surprising was that by the time they got Mr. Williams to the police station, his nerves were completely shattered and he confessed to having molested freshman girls at Thurman who were in his math class, as well as freshman girls at his previous school.

Mr. Williams' confession had come as a complete surprise to Dr. Roberts, as typically these situations took months to investigate. She had never seen a situation where the molester actually admitted his guilt. She was happy that Tanya wouldn't have to go through what could have been a long and grueling legal process. The child had been through enough. She had gotten a call from the police yesterday that Mr. Williams had gone so far as to provide them with a list of the students that he had molested, both past and present. The police told her they would make the names of the Thurman students available to the Board of Education investigators. Now the Board investigators were making the names of the students available directly to her via the fax she held in her hand.

As she walked back to her chair, her heart filled with emotion as she read the names. The paper contained the names of three girls. Tanya Neeley's name was the last on the list. The name of the student in the middle was one which Dr. Roberts didn't recognize. However, the first name on the list she recognized instantly. Mia Maldonado. She stared blankly at the page for a while longer until she finally got up and placed it in her confidential file for safekeeping until Monday. She would have to meet with these girls' parents and also see whether the girls needed any counseling.

After she closed and locked the file drawer, she sat down heavily back at her desk. Her mind drifted to Mia Maldonado and the terrible incident which resulted in her getting shot and paralyzed for life. She sat frozen at her desk for a long time as her gut churned the same question over and over again in the pit of her stomach: where had the tragedy struck first, Mia's attitude or her circumstances? Dr. Roberts knew this was a question that she would revisit in her mind for a long time.

Peering at her watch, she realized it was time for her to be on her way home for her brunch date with Reuben. Just as she reached the door to her office, she turned around to click off her light switch and noticed that the stack of papers she had found waiting for her when she arrived had metamorphosed into many small stacks spread across her desk. For a moment, it reminded her of the desk of the Wall Street attorney she used to be—a life that now seemed so distant and removed from her life with the students. Flipping off the light and pulling her office door shut, she felt herself smiling as she walked down the long hallway to the exit door. She again reflected on what Dayton Dennis had said in his commencement speech, and was glad that she had taken the opportunity to live her dream. She had chosen to be happy.

---

*http://www.webmd.com/depression/tc/seasonal-affective-disorder-sad-exams-and-tests

author's note

None of us can choose the circumstances into which we are born. We can only move forward from where we start, creating and living our own realities. However, the choice is ours how we live from one moment to the next—whether we build others up or tear them down, give or take, celebrate or envy. Life owes us nothing. It makes no promises, nor holds any guaranteed rewards. It brings joy along with disappointment, and triumph along with failure. Indeed, life is itself an oxymoron: bitterly sweet, blatantly clandestine, and relentlessly merciful.

As we stumble through times of despair, we can only hope that we take wisdom from our mistakes and find the courage to try again. Meanwhile, the one thing of which we can be certain is that between the time we take our first and last breaths, life will continue to happen to us all.

about the author

Becca Gaines Archer is a freelance writer and poet. A product of humble beginnings, she worked hard to attain a successful career as a New York City business woman and has been a dedicated community advocate. In recent years, she decided to direct her energies toward her creative side by writing her first novel, We Choose. Through her writings, she continues to drive her strong messages to encourage and inspire others. She lives with her husband in Santa Cruz, California.

www.ingramcontent.com/pod-product-compliance
Lightning Source LLC
Chambersburg PA
CBHW030522020726
47494CB00004B/1205